The Incredible Here and Now

The Incredible

Here and Now

Felicity Castagna

First published in 2013
from the Writing & Society Research Centre
at the University of Western Sydney
by the Giramondo Publishing Company
PO Box 752
Artarmon NSW 1570 Australia
www.giramondopublishing.com

© Felicity Castagna, 2013

Designed by Harry Williamson
Typeset by Andrew Davies
in 11.25 / 14 pt Garamond 3

Printed and bound by Ligare Book Printers
Distributed in Australia by NewSouth Books

National Library of Australia
Cataloguing-in-Publication data:

Castagna, Felicity
The Incredible Here and Now
ISBN 9781922146366 (pbk)

A823.4

To Zain

West

Some people say 'West' like it is something wrong, like ice-cream that fell in a gutter. I think West is like my brother's music, too much bass so you end up dancing like your body parts don't fit together and laughing all at the same time. That's what West is: shiny cars and loud things, people coming, people going – movement. Those who don't know any better, they come into the neighbourhood and lock their windows and drive on through, never stopping before they get somewhere else. But we know better. We know the boys sag their pants because they look good that way, and the fat greedy-looking guy is yelling from the balcony because his girls haven't come back from the park yet, and the men smoking hookahs at the café on the corner are only smoking stuff that smells like apples and telling each other lies like men in every other place do.

I never thought anything bad could happen here and then it did.

Everywhere People

Parramatta is an everywhere-people kind of place. People always coming and going. There's the Indian kids down the road who think they invented cricket and the Pakistani kids next door to them who are always trying to tell them they're wrong. Some people, they come from the city and some all the way from Penrith. My family, they're from somewhere else a long time ago but we've been West since the convicts landed in Parramatta Cove. Poppy says that the Raffertys in the street behind us are too loud because they're part Irish and part Italian and part Lebanese: Poppy says that's about as loud as people can get.

Mum says, when people ask you where you're from you should say, *here*, because here is where you're at. This is my mother, who says that all people from all places are good people except, maybe, the Hare Krishnas across the street who keep her awake on Sunday nights with all that wailing, but I like it because it makes me feel like I'm going to some far off place as I fall into sleep, like I'm West but I'm everywhere all at the same time.

Esther

Our apartment block is full of all kinds of people: like the lady downstairs with the name that sounds too long, who keeps vegetables in big tubs on her balcony and plays sad music on Sunday afternoons, and Omar upstairs who won't say where he comes from but I know it's not here because he showed me a picture once, of him in some desert place. There's George in the apartment behind us. He's spent his whole life in this same area, never been anywhere – never saw the point.

Esther is the best though: Esther with her half-baked chocolate-chip biscuits and her tinny cups of sherry. She lives in the bottom apartment, the one on the side behind the clothes lines and the mouldy mattress that no one admits to dumping there. When she sees me coming home from school, she yells out, 'Hey Michael. Hey!' from her window until I end up in her living room staring at her drawn-in eyebrows and her fake, old-lady pearls.

The word on Esther is that she had a son, somewhere, at some point. Mum said she saw him once hanging round the garbage tins near the left side of the apartment block. Mum said he was a thin thing, with pale blue sockets for eyes and skin like it had never seen the sun. I haven't seen him, only heard him once late at night, yelling through her window, saying he wanted some money, again and again.

That time she was all quiet-like, not Esther at all, just pleading in a small bird's voice for him to go away. I never heard her like that before, usually she's got a tongue as sharp as a knife. Dom doesn't like her so much because she always puts him in his place – like the time when he spray-painted his hair into a multi-coloured mohawk and Esther said that people would think his mother had dropped acid and had sex with a peacock.

That time, me and Esther, we just sat there laughing at Dom, growing full with a huge-arse temper until he said, 'Isn't that what happened to your son? Took too much acid or something and wandered off?'

'No,' Esther said, 'he'll be back, he'll be right.' Esther pours herself another glass of sherry with her thin shaky hands and lets it spill like she had lost hope down her dress.

School Yard

This place has its own kind of map and everyone knows which territory they belong to. Everyone knows you don't screw with the boys who sit on the steps on the way into the courtyard: the ones with the fat arms and legs whose uniforms are always tearing apart where the stitches are. Anyone with any brains knows you don't ask them to move even if they are always in the way. Eli Hanssen disappeared for three days once after he asked one of them to let him past, everyone knows that.

On the other side of the yard: there is the fat group who spend their whole lunchtime eating, the maths losers reading their textbooks and the emo retards who play Dungeons & Dragons. They're all only slightly better than the Year Sevens who play handball against the back wall and scream 'Yes!' every five minutes like they're at an Eels game and actually watching something exciting.

In the alcove outside the science block – that's where people do things they want to hide like smoking cigarettes and looking at the magazines they stole from underneath their father's closets. That's where you go if you want to act like you don't give a shit about anything and if you dyed your hair black and pierced your own ear.

Me and my best friend Shadi, we spend most of our time at the edge of the football field. Dom's group and also Shadi's cousin's group sit not so far away and because of this we're allowed to sit close but not too close to the area where all the Year Elevens and Twelves are even though we're still only in Year Ten.

Shadi's cousins sit with the Lebs. The Islanders sit a little further away than that on the other side of the field and Dom sits with the everything elses. Shadi and me, we watch everyone for most of lunchtime in between some eating and talking, but mostly we're just watching. When they leave next year we'll take over the spot. Then it'll be me and Shadi eating meat pies and chucking the wrappers at the birds, and me and Shadi chucking footballs across the field, and me and Shadi drumming, and me and Shadi talking crap and rolling each other down the hill when there's nothing more doing.

Last Day of School

In the yard, we line up in our year groups. I watch Dom, pulling faces, walking back and forth in front of the line of kids in Year 11. He's shaking his finger at them and his face is all scrunched up. He leans his tall body forward and pushes out the belly he doesn't have much of and thrusts his fingers fast through his hair like he's so pissed off he's about to explode. All the kids are laughing and you can tell, even from here, that he's doing an impersonation of Principal Alloshi. It's even funnier when Mr Alloshi gets up in front of everyone and paces back and forth with his giant pot-belly hanging over his pants, shaking his finger just like Dom.

Mr Alloshi wants to play the quiet game.

We are all allowed to leave when the whole school shows enough self-discipline to stand in silence without talking or hitting each other for five minutes. It takes forty minutes and it could've taken more if the boy standing next to Dom hadn't kicked him several times.

By the time the school gates are finally rolled open there's dozens of boys banging up against each other like car doors in an overcrowded parking lot. When the first boys get loose and make a break for the gate, there's a low howling moan that turns into a roar, their hands up in the air and everyone cheering. And then we're free as we squish ourselves through that gate, into the big hot of summer holidays.

School Holidays

Me and Dom, we work really hard at keeping busy while Mum and Dad are off at their electrical shop all day. We go raging crazy when there's nothing doing; crazy the way we steal *Best of Bollywood* videos from those spice and DVD shops crammed into the front of old houses in Harris Park. We spend hours at the park, poking around the old convict gravestones where the beer bottles stick out of the grass like some crazy kind of plant.

We wake up just after we hear everyone else leave, the door slamming behind them and then we sit on the couch, drinking instant coffee and sweetened condensed milk until we feel the rest of the day punching us in the face.

Then Dom and I walk down to Westfield and begin

the circuit. First, we go into the pet shop where Dom's girlfriend, Kate, works. We stand there, looking at the fish, pretending like we are actually going to buy some sixty-dollar fish that looks like it is growing a tumour out of its head. When the boss goes to the back for something, or is helping another customer, Kate comes over and twists the curls of her thick brown hair around her finger and leans her pokey bum against the wall and we have the same conversation we have every time.

'So, what are you boys doing today?'

'Nothin'.'

'Just hangin'.'

When the boss comes back, Kate taps her orange plastic press-on nails against the side of the tank and Dom says, 'I'll think about it then,' and we leave.

Next stop is the back of the food court in front of the fast-food places and the video-game parlour. Dom always buys us both a fifty-cent ice-cream cone from McDonald's and we sit up on the stools surveying the scene. Some of the boys from his year in school come and sit beside us. They turn their hats backward and sit low on their stools and say, 'What are you guys doing?'

'Nothin'.'

'Just hangin'.'

And the boys sit and talk for a while about who is and isn't there and what cars they're gonna get later when they save up for them.

After, we go and stand outside on the road, underneath the stairs to the cinemas where a bunch of the guys from school are smoking and making out with their girlfriends until we get bored with that too. Then we make our way down Church Street through the open mall where Dom and me dare each other to do things. We stand there for a while, watching people come and go in and out of the shops, walking out of Town Hall, walking up to the church. Dom says, 'Go over there and sit cross-legged like the Fallun-whatch-a-ma-call-it-guys' and I do, or he says 'Go dance with the Islander guys on the corner' and I do, or he says 'Go sing with the God squad' and I do.

Dom was seventeen and I was fifteen that last summer. I'd do anything he told me to. 'This,' Dom says, 'Is *the shit*.' And we walk on home not knowing things don't last forever.

Roundabouts

A 2001 Ford Falcon XR6, blue with a thin white stripe all the way down both sides of the body, worth ten times more than all the Saturdays and Sundays Dom had to work at McDonald's to buy it. When Dom first gets that car we spend the afternoons loving it; its iridescent blue paint job, the illegal blue lights he installed underneath its tray, the way Dom looks when he sits behind the wheel, the way I look flexing my muscles in front of it.

He takes us out past Granville, through Auburn and back to Church Street again. We drive in the late afternoons, after school, past the dusty little store fronts and factories long-since shut down, past the hairdressers with their old-man customers and the women with their 80s free-style hair, past the shops with their naked plastic women looking like sex.

Dom has one hand on the wheel and his head stuck out the window so that his thick hair flies back like he's in a tunnel. I have to drag him back inside again by grabbing the loose bits of his jeans. We laugh and he calms down for a minute or two and says sorry but his sorriness gets lost pretty quickly underneath the seat with his chewing gum and then we're laughing again.

We pass through the streets lined with their weather-board houses and their weak streams of lights pouring out through the metal grates of their windows and I tell myself that we are the kings of these neighbourhoods, driving through in our big fancy car, checking out what our people are doing. I watch Dom smiling his gigantic full-of-teeth smile and I know that he is dreaming the same thing and he sticks his head out the window again and I drag him back into the big safety of that car.

Making Pancakes

Dom, who doesn't even know how to boil an egg, he makes pancakes on Sunday mornings – best you've ever had anywhere.

I don't know when he learned to make them, Aunty Leena gave him the recipe once, I think, and then it became the greatest of great excuses ever.

Each time he enters the door it is the same. He comes in with half-a-dozen eggs or some sugar or sometimes a few lemons he has stolen from the house around the corner. If no one catches him coming in through the door in these early hours of Sunday morning, he puts his goods in the cupboard or hides them under the couch.

If he's caught coming in the door, he bats his eyelids and holds up a couple of eggs and says he had to go to the shop for some missing ingredient. I don't know how he gets away with it, even with his little stories, when he's standing there smelling like girls and cigarettes.

My brother the genius.

On these mornings, I sit on a stool in the kitchen and watch. Dom cracks eggs into a plastic bowl and stirs them around with a fork until they look like whipped cream. He tells me stuff quietly over butter and oil spitting in a pan. His stories are made up of different bits and pieces about cars and long nights, kids hanging out in parks smoking leaves, sniffing whip-cream cans, girls who think Dom and his friends are twenty-one not seventeen.

Dom puts on Mum's pink apron and hands me the pancakes he calls runts – the ones that come out all lopsided, a little overcooked or lumpy. By the time Mum and Dad get out of bed, I'm full of stories and pancakes and they're only just wiping the sleep out of their eyes.

Mum sits at the table, her thin body folded into her summer dressing-gown, and smiles as she watches Dom cooking in her pink apron and Dad as he gets the coffee going on the stove.

Dom brings Mum pancakes and squeezes honey over the top the way she likes it. He jabs a fork into the middle of her pancake stack so that she laughs and he says 'Eat up princess,' and pats her on the shoulder, the way that only Dom can do and everyone gets away with everything for the next hour or so, eating their fill in that apartment smelling of butter and milk and coffee.

No more space for pigeons

Poppy lives in a retirement home down the road so he is always at our place and we are always at his. Him and the old people like to sit on the lawn in plastic chairs and watch everything happening. When Poppy talks about Parramatta, it's never the one that we live in now. Poppy's Parra didn't stick around. It got lost in the tall tall buildings. Most things remind Poppy that everything's different here than it was before.

This afternoon Dom and me sit with Poppy on the lawn watching a small crane take apart two houses. It slides its arm into the side of one house and the walls just cave in like that, like they were made of nothing.

'I thought they were going to blow it up,' Dom says

to Poppy who is stretched back in his plastic chair sipping on a beer like he's watching the evening news.

Poppy shakes his head slowly. 'You don't blow up fibro. Not enough weight. The boards would blow all over the place and land in other suburbs.'

Dom scratches at his knees and looks disappointed. 'What happened to the pigeons?'

Of the houses that are left in this area, this was Dom and me's favourite because of the pigeons. The man who owned the place kept them in big cages out the back and only let them out in the evenings when they flew in a V-shape around the neighbourhood and then circled back towards his house again. Dom and me asked him about it once and he said he raced them against each other. He liked to let the pigeons go from all other places around the city and timed how long it took them to get home.

'No more space for things like pigeons anymore. Only apartments. There weren't any apartments here you know when your parents first got married. They lived in a fibro too and I lived in one of the square brick houses – they built dozens of them, after the war.'

In less than twenty minutes the house is gone. First, the crane lands on top of the roof and smashes through the tiles, then it pulls apart the walls, then we're staring at its inside rooms. I look for the pigeon man in his private spaces but he's gone too. There's nothing there but grey-brown carpet and bits of wood and bits of tiles and then that disappears and the whole house turns into a pile of matchsticks.

Dom and me and Poppy, we just keep on staring.

Poppy sips his beer and runs his spotty hand over his bald head and frowns. He looks at the space where the pigeon man lived and says, 'Everything has to be too modern-looking now.'

Postie-bike

Once, a few years ago, Poppy brought an old postie-bike he'd found dumped down an alleyway back to the home and took it apart on the front lawn. He removed each part as carefully as I'd seen him pick horses from the guide at the races. I watched him as he crouched down, bending his big solid body over the bike. He looked at that bike's insides for ages before slowly pushing himself up with one hand on his knee and the other hand wrapped around some greasy black piece of metal he pulled out of the bike's body. It looked like he was planting a garden of brake pads and engine bolts. Everyone in the street came out to watch him at some point over the next few days he stationed himself there; my eighty-year-old grandfather with his dreams of speed. When he was finished, Poppy took Dom and me for rides around the neighbourhood wearing our bike helmets. I told him to slow down but every time I did, he'd just lift his hand and wave my suggestion off, so I stopped saying it after a while – mostly to keep his hands where they should be.

We hugged Parramatta River, heading out towards Harris Park. The water in the lake looked like shredded metal. Maybe it was the speed and the air on my brain but there was definitely something about that day that made the river look so much more real than it usually did.

When we headed back, we went past the car yards and the motorcycle shops. And I knew that he was just showing off in his own way, to all people working there, never noticing him.

We came back through Church Street, slowly. It is always backed up. You don't go there to get anywhere quickly. That's not the point. Poppy drove us down it and we became part of the daily parade; lowered Hondas driven by boys with mullet cuts and the hijab-covered mums in their Corollas and the bikies just pulling up and parking on the sidewalk because they can. We were part of all that, me and Poppy.

The Fast and The Furious

Dom tells everyone that he's named after Dominic Toretto from *The Fast and The Furious* movies. That's a lie, but all of Dom's boys think it's pretty cool of our mum. Even though Dom was born like seven years before the first movie came out and even though Mum makes a point of rolling her eyes at car movies and even though she's always saying, 'Aren't you boys interested in anything else?' whenever she sees us watching something with fast cars bursting into flames. And even though all of this, the boys still believe Dom.

It's only the third week of the school holidays and already Dom and me have watched all *The Fast and The Furious* films, four times, and beat each other a hundred times on the Xbox game. It's basically the same story but sometimes the hot chicks and the buff guys are in America and sometimes they're in Brazil or Tokyo or some island no one's ever heard of. And wherever they are, they've got nitrous-oxide containers strapped to their backs like torpedoes shoved up their arses.

When we're exhausted from all the fastness, Dom makes us ice-coffee with the International Roast Mum has in the cupboard and a can of sweetened condensed milk. We go out to the balcony for our first bit of outside air for the day and we watch the people driving up and down our street. Our street is long and straight with not so many stop signs and because of all this, guys like to come and see how fast their cars can go. Dom and I watch this pearly white Pontiac Trans Am going up and down the street. We've seen the car before, Dom loves it. He smiles, leans over the balcony and wipes the sweat from his forehead with the back of his arm.

Dom loves Fords. He's a 'nothin' but Ford' man. He quotes Dominic Toretto, 'I live my life a quarter mile at a time, nothing else matters. For those ten seconds or less...I'm free.'

Driving East

Me and Dom in the car: Dom sits low in the seat with his black cap on backwards and we head; we don't talk. We're heading to Jane's party: Jane with the big house in Rose Bay, who told everyone on Facebook that her parents are on holidays.

We head East. The night is full-up with the red tail-lights of cars and the rims of hubcaps. Dom turns on the CD player, something harsher than he usually listens to. Dom broke up with Kate yesterday so his feelings are all fucked up. He's not smiling all the time like he usually does. They'll get back together tomorrow, anyway, they always do.

'Plenty of fish in the sea,' I say, like Mum does but it

comes out all awkward and stupid-sounding the way I say it.

He turns his eyes off the road for a few seconds and looks at me a bit worried-like. It's not the sort of reaction I was expecting and it makes me feel kind of powerful and kind of bad for him all at the same time.

When we get to Granville, we pick up four of Dom's friends on the corner. James gets in the front between us so he's shoving his elbow in my face to get some room and when I look in the rear-view mirror it's just a jumble of legs and arms and big chests and I pick out the faces of David and Yousef and Mark. And everyone is laughing and talking loudly. And then suddenly, and for no reason at all, they start chanting, 'Jane is game... Jane is game.'

And Dom is beginning to smile so I start chanting it, even though I don't know what it means, but *it is* kind of funny and you can tell that everyone is feeling good.

When we get to the East it's hard to find the right place because the streets are all wrapped around themselves. In the places you do not live things look imaginary like you're going off into another world. Everything is one way and then two again and all the houses are big but scrunched up next to each other and the house numbers are hidden behind rose bushes.

When we find the place, it looks like the set of a movie. There are girls everywhere. They all have tight pony-tails and tighter jeans. Everyone in the East is plainer. The girls wear less makeup and the boys are thinner and blonder. It works out great at first because Dom and his friends grab everyone's attention like Dominic Toretto and his crew in *The Fast and The Furious*, walking through the party with their wide shoulders and their smaller waists so they all look like giant Vs with heads on top. I'm like the undercover cop that's always hanging out with the crew – smaller, more freckles, thinner hair – but I still manage to look good on account of who I'm with.

But then all these boys move in and around us. These boys have that stiff kind of hair from too much sea and warm-brown skin like they've got the beach inside them. They begin to follow us around and ask stuff like, 'Where do you come from?' and 'How do you know Jane?' and 'How come you didn't bring any girls of your own?' And then suddenly one of them is standing over David and he's saying, 'Granville. Isn't that where rapists come from?'

I start to feel all hot around my neck and the words, 'Jane is game' burst out of me like a chewing gum bubble. Dom looks at me and laughs and so does David and then we're pissing ourselves and we just can't stop and then these people, they don't matter so much anymore.

Chicken

We drop Dom's friends off at the corner and get to the eating. Late nights are what charcoal chicken is for. The shop is crammed with men in their neon-coloured shirts coming off a shift and old guys from the pub across the road that's shut for the night. Everyone's looking stuffed from work or too much beer. They hang their bodies over the chairs so that their legs jut out under other people's tables. Men stretch their arms above their heads.

Behind the counter, there's a wall of chickens turning around growing brown and dark: a man sprays them with the bottle of oil in his right hand and wipes the sweat from his forehead with the left.

We sit at one of the plastic tables in the corner, just

silent-like, listening to the Arab pop tunes on the big TV in the corner and the men smacking their lips together, shoving their food down. Our half-a-chicken comes with the lot, pink pickles and green ones, bundles of mint and green olives and tomatoes and dips.

Dom is the chicken sandwich master. He tears off a slice of Lebanese bread and shoves it so full of stuff that you'd think everything's gonna fall out but it doesn't. He eats the whole thing in three mouthfuls and goes to make another. Me, I've got garlic sauce rolling down my arm before the food even gets in my mouth. I lick it off the inside of my arm: it tastes salty and creamy and sweet.

These are the best times. When it's just silence between us, I know everything's good. We sit back in our chairs and eat and watch the street. Even at this time of night there's things going on. I watch three men standing on a street corner, their arms around each other, looking at their feet, mumbling. One man raises his head and laughs, he's got half a beard growing and big hands like my father's: he slaps someone else on the back and they all get to laughing again.

And then, all of a sudden, Dom is standing, standing with no sound, one hand on his hip, the other holding up his chicken sandwich, a big grin on his face. I turn to what he's looking at and it's that big pearly white Pontiac Trans Am floating down the street in slow motion like it owns the place.

Dom moves over towards the glass walls of the shop to get a better look. I take my mobile out and get a picture as quickly as I can but I just get its tail-lights and Dom, side-on, with a mad smile and a chicken sandwich and the yellow glow of those lights bright on his face.

Esther's Son

When Dom and I get back to the apartment it's late. We park the Falcon in the alleyway next to our apartment so that Dom can see it from the window of his room. Next to where we park, there's this guy sitting in the gutter. We sit for a few minutes and I can tell Dom's nervous about leaving his car, so we both stay there for a while in the dark and besides, whoever wants to go home anyway?

Dom stretches his arms out, the muscles look firm and tanned. One day I want to have huge-arse arms too. He puts the radio on. It's Eminem's 'Lose Yourself'. Dom starts first and then I can't help myself. 'You better lose yourself in the music, the moment, you own it.' Dom puts his arm up on the window and rests it there like he's a gangster. He starts to make these big, bobbing head moves like Eminem does in his Slim Shady videos. His shaggy brown hair jumps up and down on his head.

I laugh so hard I fart. 'You're never, ever going to be able to pick up, little brother,' Dom says cracking a window and a smile at the same time.

I put my arm up on my window and bob my head up and down real hard until it gives me a headache and I have to stop. I switch off the music to stop my head from aching and I realise that the guy in the gutter is calling 'Mum, Mum,' loud enough so that it's almost a shout but probably not so loud that someone in the apartment block can hear him.

I listen to the man and I think, *this is what lonely is*. Dom says, 'That's him, that's Esther's son.' I don't look at him. I couldn't, even if I wanted to. I imagine Esther behind the wall, alone at her kitchen table, eating something boring, drinking sherry. Outside her apartment things go on without her: kids make out in the park, people are sitting in their cars with the music too loud and her son sits in the gutter looking up at the sky.

Dom, Mum, Me

Sunday afternoons in summer right before the storms come, Mum wants her boys to take her out for some fresh air. Me and Dom and Mum, we walk down Parramatta River. Dom slips his arm underneath Mum's and walks her like he's a gentleman. He's taller than her now by almost a head and it makes her look even smaller when she is walking beside him. She has her blond hair pulled into a long ponytail and I can picture that her and Dad probably looked this way once, Dad with his dark features and blue eyes like Dom, and Mum looking like the colour of corn all over. I pick up flat pebbles and try to skip them across the river as we walk.

Mum likes to hear everyone's stories, not just our

own, but stories about our friends and their families, our neighbours, the people we meet on the street while she's at work.

Dom tells Mum about the pearly white Pontiac Trans Am that goes up and down the street in the middle of the day when no one is around to watch it except him. He thinks it's a sign. He imagines himself in the same sort of car one day. He's got a plan to save, to get his mate to paint it, to order some of the parts cheaper from China.

Mum presses her thin lips together and says, 'Well, you better get a good job first. Finish school, get a good job and then maybe later you'll have a bit of cash to blow on things you don't need.'

'Don't need!?' Dom says stumbling back like Mum has just shot him in the chest.

Mum grabs his arm and holds him close against her body, 'You and your cars,' she says, 'you drive me crazy.'

We walk up to the ferry station and pause to watch a ferry come in through the bushes. Not much of school holidays left now. Mum and Dom and me lean against the rail and the wind hits us in the face. I tell Mum about Esther's son sitting out in the gutter looking lonely. She pats my back and nods and we walk and she says, 'That's just how it is sometimes when families break up.' But I don't know: I can't imagine it. You break up with girls (like Dom does) but I don't know how you break up with family.

Hair Art

This afternoon, Kate comes with us, she doesn't say much, just hangs off Dom like she's his extra arm. We walk up to Phillip Street where there's the row of hairdressers all whacked up beside each other. The hairdressers hang outside in the street, sitting on milk crates, leaning against the glass walls of their shops, smoking, running their hands through their mullet cuts and shaved heads with Nike logos cut into them.

We stand in front of the shops looking at the pictures in their windows. There's photos of tough-looking guys with mohawks and boys with plaited rats' tails. Dom is staring at the pictures of the guys with stars and zig-zaggy patterns shaved into their undercuts. 'That,' he says, 'is what I'm getting.' He points to an image of a man with a thin carpet of hair running from his forehead to the back of his neck. On each side, he's got a diamond pattern shaved into his head. 'Mum's gonna kill you,' I say but I know he'll do it anyway and I know he'll get away with it.

Inside, the itchy smell of fresh-cut hair gets up my nose. There's four stools in the tiny shop and Dom and Kate take the two that aren't already taken. There's a fat man getting his hair shaved off while he eats Chinese take-away and a younger guy who wants the hairdresser to put his razor on three different settings; one for the top, one for the sides, one for the back.

There's two big mirrors and a bunch of small glass coffee cups lying around on the floor. Women don't come here. They only use clippers. The fanciest thing you can get is those patterns shaved into the side of your head.

The hairdresser throws a towel around Dom's neck and tucks it into the back of his shirt. He's got three different razors strapped to his belt and he gets each out one by one, stopping every few minutes to stand back and admire his work like he's an artist or something. Kate pulls her stool up next to Dom and holds his hand through the whole thing like it's major surgery. I watch them in the mirror. Dom is concentrating real hard on the lines emerging on his head. His square jaw is locked and his eyebrows are pushing together. Kate is licking her fat pink lips as if she's going to eat him when it's all over. As usual, she's got too much red on her cheeks and black eyeliner around her eyes so that she always looks kind of shocked.

When he's done he kicks Dom's loose hair under the chair and everyone in the shop comes to have a look. Dom runs his fingers down the side of his head and looks in the mirror as if he's done real good work. When he gets up he stands next to the guy who shaved him and without looking at each other they both pull their pants down slightly so that the belt is around the hips not on top of it and they're sagging just enough to look good. I try to pull down my pants a little too, but it never looks right. I haven't got enough hips or arse to keep my jeans down but also stop them from falling around my ankles.

'What do you think?' Dom says to me in the mirror. 'I think Mum's gonna kill you,' I say but we're both smiling because we know he looks great, whatever Mum says.

Ice-skating

Dom always calls it ice-skating, ice-skating but with cars. Sometimes, late in the evening, we go up near Lake Parramatta when there aren't too many people about and take his car ice-skating after our parents have gone to sleep. Up here, the roads are wide open and the houses all sit like lonely leftovers in their squat concrete blocks.

Dom lets me drive sometimes but tonight I'm in the back-middle seat. Dom's driving and his girlfriend's sitting in the front next to him with her hand on his leg. 'Faster,' she calls out and I can see her grabbing his leg more tightly. Dom speeds up and drives another few blocks before hitting the brakes. We slide forward for what feels like forever. The concrete turns into a plain of smooth ice below the tires of the car.

'You're crazy,' his girlfriend calls out. He turns up Dr Dre on the radio and I watch from the back as Dom rubs her knee and inches his hand up closer between her legs. Dom gets all the girls. I don't get any but I like to watch Dom so that I can learn something I might be able to use later.

'Time for a drink?' his girlfriend calls out, passing their bottle of vodka to the back seat of the car. I take it, holding the neck of the bottle with one hand. I suck down the thrill of it. It has the taste of her lipstick still on the rim. I imagine this is what sex tastes like, kind of sticky and sweet and burning with the aftertaste of Listerine.

When I hand it back, she looks hot and excited like she's ready for the future to keep coming and coming. 'Figure eights,' Dom calls out and suddenly we are swerving into the front of someone's yard and back again and back. I watch the trees just standing there at the side of the road. They look at me, shocked.

I lean forward between them and watch as Dom's girlfriend pours the vodka into her mouth: it streams out from the sides of her lips as the car swings around.

Dom drives faster, hits the brakes and turns the wheel hard. The world goes into slow motion. We pirouette again and again and suddenly I feel as though I am watching the whole thing from outside of my own body looking back at myself. Dom's girlfriend is screaming. Dom is laughing. I am outside of myself and then – literally – I am on the outside. I feel my body fly through the windscreen, landing on someone's lawn with a thud, the bone in the arm I land on snaps apart like a twig.

Concrete

The first thing I see is Mum praying. This is after all the spinning stops and the pain wakes me up in this white room. She is kneeling at the edge of my bed, her face an ashtray of smudged black circles.

There is a sinking feeling inside of me, like there's concrete in my chest and I'll never be able to get up again with the weight of it. I look around the room for Dom but he's not there. It's just Mum, Aunty Leena, Dad and Poppy. Their red puffy eyes. Tears. I try to remember how to speak.

I look out the window where summer is: hot, hot, hot, even the breeze this time of year is skin-melting. When a body appears behind the window I know that it's Dom by the way he tilts his head, slightly to the left. He's got his hands tucked into the pockets of his jeans. I can see he's not offering any kind of sadness, he's just saying goodbye.

I watch Dom from behind, as he walks away, jeans sagging, and disappears into some part of the sky. I want to say sorry but the word is stuck in the concrete in my chest. And I know that my life isn't *my life* any more: It is like a movie, it's the place where I enter the scene again and everything is different.

Fist

Every time I wake up in the hospital there is someone sitting there in my white, white room. First thing, I have to remind myself that I am alive, next thing – that Dom is not. I want to crawl back into the dark in my head but my dad is sitting there so I keep my eyes open just for him.

He reaches his two hands up and puts them around mine. One of his hands is all purple and swollen. There are cuts on the knuckles, places where the blood has dried out and turned black. I look at his hand and I try to get the information right in my head again. Was Dad in the accident? No. It was me, Dom, Kate. The car. Ice-skating. Trees. The night. Black roads. I am here. Dom is not. Kate?

I look at Dad's hands again. One is fine. One is not.

He's still got both his hands wrapped around my right hand. He leans his whole body up against the bed and looks at me real hard. I can see his eyes looking at my hair and then my nose and then my ears and then my cheeks, like he's making sure that every bit of my head is still in the right place.

I try to lift my head. I want to sit up all the way. If I could sit up things would make more sense. Things would be more clear. I only manage to lift myself a little bit more when my dad snaps his head up straight like all of a sudden he's seen a ghost or something.

He puts his cold swollen hand on my head and whispers *shhh,* even though I haven't said anything. I watch his face. He is growing dark hairs in patches around his chin and his cheeks. 'How could this happen?' he says, but I don't think he's really asking me a question.

He looks away from me and out the window.

Do you know the meaning of words?

This time when I wake up Mum is there. She is silent, not looking at me, I want to tell her how it happened, how Dom was smiling, how that smile was the last thing he was, but it is so hard to put the whole story into words. My tongue doesn't know the language but my body can feel it. Sometimes I am not sure if it really did happen but then I can feel it again in the heaviness of my chest.

Heavy: it is the only word I can think of to tell the story. If I could find the right words, I could store our grief in them. I could let it go out my mouth and into the air.

First Day, New World

Poppy waits in front of the hospital with me. He is holding the string of a big red balloon that floats above his head. It says *Get Well Soon*. I think it's meant for me but he's forgotten to hand it over. Dad brings the car around and we both get in.

No one talks on the short drive back home. I look out the car window. Everything looks empty and still, like everyone has just packed up and gone home. There's no music coming out of car windows or people talking too loudly on street corners or cars revving up in the distance. There's nothing.

When we arrive at our apartment, Poppy gets out of the front and comes around to the back of the car and opens up the door for me. He's still holding the balloon. 'I forgot,' he says. 'This one's for you.' Dad is sitting in the driver's seat not moving. Poppy smiles at me but you can tell it's not a real smile. It's too wide and he's showing all his yellowing teeth, even the gap where he's missing a tooth on his left side. He grabs the plastic bags of bears and posters and chocolates and things from the hospital that are sitting next to me. He gives me the balloon in return.

Upstairs, Dad unlocks the door and Poppy goes in first, walking down the hallway where Dom's shoes are still lying on their side like they always are. Dad holds the door open for me and says 'It's good to have you back,' in a voice that is softer than I've heard him use before. In the hallway, just near the front door there is a hole in the wall that I've never seen before. Dad sees me looking and his cheeks go red. He puts his banged-up hand in his pocket. I look at the hole again.

'Coffee, I'll make coffee.' I hear Poppy say this from the kitchen right before I hear the sound of him opening the fridge and pulling back the tab on a can of beer.

Dad and I sit down on the couch and he puts his arm around me. Poppy brings in two cans of beer and a glass of lemonade for me. 'Can't be bothered with coffee today,' he says sitting on the recliner. He looks tired, real tired, like he's just been running marathons. I look at Dad sipping his beer beside me and he looks real tired too.

'Where's Mum?'

Poppy and Dad look at each other for a while until Poppy gets that weird fake smile again and says, 'The doctor gave her something to help her sleep better. We'll just let her sleep now and you can talk to her tomorrow.'

I sip at my lemonade and we all lie back into the couch. Poppy puts his feet up on the coffee table and rubs his belly. Dad rubs his eyes. The clock on the wall says it is four.

The Other Side

Now, everything is different. Mum is in bed or sometimes she's out of bed but she looks like she's sleep-walking and Dad is acting calm and saying positive things but his hands are always swollen and there is another hole in the wall that came out of nowhere.

I'm sitting on a plastic chair on the lawn with Poppy when I break.

'Stop it!' I say too loud and too close to his head so that he sits up quickly and spills some of the beer in his can onto his pants.

'What?'

'That fake kind of smile when you look at me. You look like a tool.' It's the first time I've ever said anything like that to Poppy. He leans forward towards me with both hands on his knees and he's got this half-arsed grin where the right side of his mouth is all pushed up and he says, 'I'm a tool? Like a screwdriver or a hammer…or a bandsaw?'

I'm trying not to laugh. I'm angry but he's funny. 'No, like you look like a retard. Everyone's acting all fake and stupid.'

He drags his chair over closer to mine and puts his arm around my shoulder. He sips his beer and we watch the concrete being poured for the apartment building going up across the road.

'Okay,' Poppy says. He's still watching the building. Still sipping at his beer. 'Everyone is just trying to do their best you know. Your dad, your mum, me. It's hard to know how you're meant to help each other, how you're meant to act. Hard to know how you go on doing anything.'

'Yeh,' I say. It's the only response I want to give. For now, I just don't want to look at his face. I want to watch the men smoothing out the concrete with a rake and I want to try and think about nothing.

This Place

This day, I'm needing to be with somebody so I'm out looking for Shadi. It's kind of like looking for someone in one of those *Where's Wally* books. He could be out just pissin' around on a street corner with one of his ninety cousins so you've got to look all around the north-side, the south-side and the east-side where Parramatta borders with Harris Park and then out to Granville. This whole place is marked off in so many different territories and I know them all so well sometimes it feels like the place isn't big enough, like you just can't get beyond it. I get on my bike and start riding.

I ride down to the sports grounds around Parramatta Leagues where the stadium and the swimming pool is;

where the local kids have turned the parking lot into an unofficial skate-park. I scan the crowds of guys trying to sag their too-tight jeans and the girls watching them skate.

Down the road I ride through Prince Alfred Park where the homeless guys are getting their afternoon tea from the food van that comes and pulls up there...But Shadi's not around, hanging in the rotunda with the other kids, trying to get the homeless men to buy them beer. So I ride on through, down Church Street, not stopping because I know I shouldn't be riding my bike between all the customers spilling out onto the street, having their afternoon glass of wine and their plates of mixed stuff.

When I ride up towards Westfield he's not there either in the open mall where everyone comes from everywhere just to hang out, so I ride on up to Little China Town and stare at the skinned ducks hanging upside-down in the shop windows.

Everything in my body still hurts but I don't really care. Everyone's out today, so I have to try not to knock anyone over as I ride past. They're out with their shopping bags and their boxes full of Asian greens and their sets of magnum hubcaps from Auto Alley. I want to push through them all until I find Shadi somewhere standing on a street corner behind them.

My Father's Hands

My father, he wakes up in the dark tired and gets up anyway. He combs his hair with water and goes to his electrical shop before everyone is out of bed. He is always on his way somewhere, always telling everyone that things will turn out all right.

Dad thinks it's better now that I spend more time with him working in the shop. He says that we need to be strong, that we need to keep it together for Mum's sake. I get up when I hear him walking into the kitchen and pull my jeans and shirt on. We don't talk until we're out of the house, walking down the street. He buys us sweet bread and takeaway coffees in styrofoam cups from the Persian store on the way. 'How ya goin' kiddo,' he says as we're walking down the street.

I say 'Fine,' bread crumbling out the sides of my mouth.

'Big year for you,' he says, 'Almost Year Eleven, then you'll be doing your HSC. Before you know it you'll be going places.'

I nod. I'm not sure about all this, not sure I really care or that I know what places I want to be going. My dad goes all silent and I know he's thinking about Dom.

When we get to the shop tucked up in its little alleyway off of Church Street, he pulls across the metal grate and I try to make sense of the graffiti someone's written on the wall overnight.

Inside he hands me a jack-knife and I help him tear off the tops of boxes packed tight with their odd collections of electrical plugs and styrofoam.

We sit behind the counter together, me sorting the random bits and pieces into different boxes to be put on the shelf and sold. My father sits there putting together and taking apart the miniature electric arm he has been building for the last week. I stop what I'm doing and watch him for a while. 'What are you doing?'

'I'm making something that could reach into tight places and fix things, like perhaps the insides of machines, maybe in a factory.'

I keep on watching him, my father with his big strong hands, and his purple bashed-up knuckles, moving all these small objects into tight places, always inventing, always wanting to be hopeful.

Aunty Leena

So. This is how it goes. Aunty Leena and I were in the park all day. I was pulling up too-small fish from Parramatta River. Aunty Leena's son, Sam sat by my side *ooing* and *ahhing* at everything I pulled up. I never get anything big enough to take home, really, but I keep at it anyway. And besides, I like being with Aunty Leena. She listens to me like she really gets it even when she's sitting there in her short-shorts fanning herself with copies of *Woman's Day* and *Cosmopolitan*.

When Aunty Leena dropped me home, I'd forgotten about the mud on my shoes. By the time Mum actually stood up from her position on the couch and looked at the floor, I had trampled little half-moons of dirt all the way from the front door to the kitchen and back to the living room again.

When she folded her arms and looked at me, I tried to give her a wide-eyed blink, like I didn't quite understand – just like Dom used to do. My brother could get away with anything but me, nope, can't even look sideways at something interesting before Mum's eyes are darting at me.

She doesn't know anything Mum, not about my brother I mean, wouldn't have a clue about the box full of magazines buried in the park across the road or how the good china teapot she inherited from her great aunt suddenly disappeared. Lots of other stuff I could tell her about if I really wanted to.

I say, 'I'm sorry, I forgot,' and she mutters something about Aunty Leena never doing the right thing before she gets out a sponge and starts scrubbing.

Her and Aunty Leena haven't been right since Aunty Leena got caught pole dancing at The Roxy two weeks after my brother's death. The only excuse Aunty Leena gave was, 'You can take the girl out of Blacktown but you can't take Blacktown out of the girl.' This is Aunty Leena's primary reasoning for a lot of things, like wearing too much makeup or saying the wrong things at the wrong time.

We all have our own excuses. Dom's excuses were his unusually deep blue eyes, the ones he used to wink at all the girls on the bus going home from school, those eyes that got as large as steering wheels when he came home way after curfew and our mother was standing there in the hallway. No one could tell him no. Not with those eyes.

Staring

First day of school. There's the noise of everyone shouting and talking as I reach the door of homeroom and then there's just nothing. They're all sitting there in silence like it's normal.

All eyeballs are on me, except when I stare back at someone and they pretend to be concentrating really hard on the gum stuck underneath their desk. I wonder if this is what it will be like from now on: if I'll spend the rest of the school year with their eyeballs chewing into my skull.

Shadi and The Pool

Shadi and I are always at the pool on those too-hot Saturday mornings towards the end of summer. We walk in with the four towels and two grocery bags full of food that Shadi's mother has given us just in case we get hungry. We set up our spot just under one of the trees and scope the place out like we hadn't come here yesterday, the day before, the day before that.

The sign that runs the pool always has something new on it. As well as 'No Diving, No Running, No Eating in the Pool', 'No Lebs' has been written in and crossed out, 'No Rangas' has been written in and crossed out, 'No Asians with gangsta tatoos' has been written in and crossed out, until everyone has decided on the one thing they can all agree on. 'No Fat Chicks.' It stays there like a warning to all the girls pulling their bikini bottoms out of their bum cracks and nervously sucking in their bellies.

Shadi takes off his shirt and rubs the bit of his belly that's hanging over his waistband. He stares at the grass and grins. He's always grinning like he can see secrets everywhere or something. 'Think I'll have something to eat first,' he says sitting down, rummaging through the bags of food.

'Right,' I say, 'I'm going in.'

Shadi grunts at me, his mouth already filled with Leb bread.

I walk over to the shallow end and slowly slip myself in. In the corner there are a few of the girls I recognise from around the block. They're just wading around in the water, trying not to get their hair and their makeup all messed up. I look at them and smile, and one of them, the one with the thick brown curly hair, smiles back. I watch her stick her head under the water and swim across the pool. She's the only one of the girls that doesn't seem to care about getting her face and her hair all messed up. When she pops her head above the water again her hair and her face are all shiny like she's a car hood that's been waxed down. She looks over at me again real quick like she doesn't want me to notice her noticing me. None of the girls ever pays much attention to me and Shadi when we're here, but a smile or two and we'll have something to talk about later on the walk home.

I stick my head under the water and try to make my way through all the legs and arms for a while, ducking my head in and out. Everything above is loud and bright, everything below – just whispers.

When I look over towards Shadi, he's making his flabby way over to the pool. That's when two guys from school come over and knock him straight backwards on the pavement. By the time I swim over towards him, they're sitting on his chest so that the wind has flown completely out of him and he's lying there, gasping in pockets of air.

Before I can reach him, there's this skinny woman life-guard rushing over with a megaphone, yelling at the two boys to get off and remove themselves from the pool grounds.

Me and the woman life guard take each of Shadi's arms and help him back over to the tree. She puts her hand on his chest and tells him to breathe, breathe slowly, and I watch as Shadi breathes again and smiles. And I know he's smiling because this woman is standing there in her swimmers touching his chest and I worry that he'll start hyperventilating with the excitement of it all.

When she leaves, Shadi's still smiling. I hit him in the shoulder and say, 'You alright?' and he keeps on smiling through his wheezing.

After we've been sitting under the tree for a while, that girl comes over: the brown-haired wax girl from the pool. She's wrapped herself up in her towel like it's a dress and she comes and sits next to me, pushing her knees up underneath her chin and says, 'Your friend alright?'

'Yeh,' I say looking at the creamy bits of her knees under her chin.

'Yeh,' Shadi chimes in and we all look out to the water for a while, watching where her friends are looking at us.

'I'm Mo,' she says, 'short for Monique,' and me and Shadi just keep staring at her, until we remember to introduce ourselves too. Shadi pulls out three of the cans of Coke his mother has packed us and gives us each one.

She puts the cold can to her forehead and rubs it down her cheeks.

'Hot?'

'Yeh real hot,' she says and I roll my can of Coke down her arm, and she lets me, and I feel like the world is full of possibilities.

Communion

Outside, everyone hangs around the courtyard of St Pat's, just talking before the ceremony begins. It's Sam's first communion and we all go along even though my Poppy keeps reminding us he's a bastard – a bastard that we love, but a bastard none the less. He's never quite forgiven Aunty Leena for bringing this child into the world, a child with a father, somewhere, that none of us has ever met. Aunty Leena introduces Dad and Mum and Poppy and me to all the other parents, 'This is my nephew,' she says, 'handsome little lady killer, and this is my sister-in-law, best cook in the West, and this is my brother, the great inventor.' Aunty Leena is the type of person that makes everyone feel good about themselves. She has this way of making you feel like whoever you are, you're the best thing you could be.

But I'm not paying much attention to all that. I look at the statue of the Virgin Mary. I always liked looking at what she was holding. People put all sorts of weird stuff in her hands at different times of the year – chocolates, rosary beads, a toy car – sometimes people tie ribbons around her wrists. At Dom's funeral she was holding a small bunch of flowers.

I look for my mum but she's not outside with the crowds. When I go back into the church I see that she's kneeling there, praying silently by herself. After Dom died I remember her like this for days, praying with her rosary beads in her hands, turning them over and over again. All the women from the church came to pray with her that time. They prayed so hard it was like the whole Cathedral rocked.

At those times I sat outside here in the courtyard. I didn't want to look at all the people's faces, I didn't want them looking at me. So, instead, I sat out there with the Virgin Mary, both of us as heavy as concrete.

Bells ring. At some point everyone starts moving towards the big Cathedral doors. Poppy is beside me, his big rectangle of a body hovering. Sam's with the other children standing at the back of the Cathedral, dressed up in their miniature suits and veils.

We sit and wait as the kids all take their first

confessions. I watch Sam standing in line, looking nervous, shoving his fists as deep as he can into his little suit pockets. When he's about to get his first communion wafer I give him the thumbs up. He looks back to me and returns the gesture instead of doing the sign of the cross and Aunty Leena laughs. Mum glares and whispers, 'Stop distracting him,' so I get to distracting Poppy instead, he's closed his eyes and is slouching forward. I punch him in the ribs a little too hard and he sits up again with a long loud 'Owww', so that everyone in the pews in front of us turns around and glares.

When the service is over, the double doors of the Cathedral are opened. The daylight falls between the people passing through the doors. It was bright when the service began; now the sky is dark.

Girl with No Name

Dom's old girlfriend used to have lots of huge-arse hair. Now she's cut it short so she looks all fierce. Sometimes I see her at the shops. We don't look at each other, not directly, not since the funeral when she cried so hard her father had to carry her out of the church.

She's looking at the rack with the chips and pretzels. I watch her pick up each packet and run a long red nail over the foil as if she is speed-reading the ingredients on the back. We stand close. She's got that heaviness hanging over her too. She knocks a packet to the floor and leaves it there. She knocks another one down and pushes past me and I can feel it – her hunger, her disappointment, her rage.

I watch her walk up to the counter with a packet of

Lifesavers. I watch the slight bend of her shoulders and I want to go up and touch her, tell her *I'm sorry, I'm sorry all the time*.

But whenever I see her, I can't ever look her straight in the face. I can't even say her name.

Wallpaper

I don't exactly know when Mum slipped out of our lives. I think I just looked up one day and she'd become a part of the wall, sitting there in the corner of the shop, or in the living room, her dress blending into the wallpaper.

Today, I only noticed her because she moved, detaching herself from the grey wall of my father's shop – the shock of seeing her passes through me like a lightning bolt and I say, 'Hey Mum,' calling from my position in front of the keyboards I am dusting.

'Morning,' she says even though it is getting close to the afternoon. 'I'll make us something to eat.'

'Good. Great,' I imitate the language of my father, always positive, always encouraging. I stand at the door to the tiny staff room and watch her moving without sound, pouring drinks that don't splash, leaving her fingerprints on sandwich bread so that you know she's really there.

'Thanks.'

We sit there chewing and chewing until Aunty Leena comes through the door. She dumps her handbag down behind the counter and goes straight over to a customer who's just walked in and is looking at the two squat, past-their-use-by-dates microwaves in the back corner. My mum never wanted to hire Aunty Leena but even she's had to admit that Aunty Leena's pretty good at it. Aunty Leena can sell anything, walking around the shop in her tight jeans and high heels. I watch her from the storeroom and I know exactly what she's doing. She's not trying to rope in a customer, she's trying to get one out. It's Bill, one of the guys who lives under the rotunda in the park across the road. Lost his marbles ages ago my dad says, but he still knows everything there is to know about microwaves and insists he's in the market for one. Aunty Leena locks her arm in his and says, 'That's amazing Bill, radiation you say. We'll have to talk about it again some other time,' as she walks him straight outside the door and waves him goodbye while he's still talking.

Back inside the shop, Aunty Leena and me and Mum spend the afternoon sorting out adapter plugs. Aunty Leena and I joke, dropping the plugs into little boxes marked China-Australia, Australia-Lebanon. My mum spends most of the afternoon puzzling over a couple of plugs, like she'll forget to breathe if she has to concentrate on anything else. It's these kind of times that she can't look at me, when I know she's really missing him.

Aunty Leena eventually gets up and hugs Mum from behind and I stand there, holding my arms out, like a bucket for her sadness, knowing I'm not enough to contain it.

Walking in Different Ways

Dad walks me to school the other way. Not past the Coke factory, the way all the boys go, but his kind of way through Parramatta Park. He likes to walk past all the old buildings and underneath the fig trees on the bicycle path. He walks and does not say anything. His heavy feet make the stones on the ground fly up around his shoes. The park is different in the morning. No one is around playing footy or cricket the way they do in the afternoons or drinking at night. This time of day it's mums with prams and guys with pot bellies jogging.

Dad stops at the bubbler and has a drink. When he straightens up he wipes the back of his hand against his mouth. He looks at me again, like he's making sure that all my arms and legs are still in the right place. I don't ask him why he's walking me to school for the first time since I was ten. He takes a deep breath and swallows hard as if he needs to make himself feel okay again.

These are days of silence and swimming pools and feeling like concrete on the inside.

Laughter

Mum, Dad, Poppy, Aunty Leena, Sam and me are sitting on the balcony having some food when we hear a huge noise like metal collapsing on metal. When we all lean over the balcony, it's Esther there, dressed in her nightgown still, showing a bit too much flesh, rollers falling out of her hair. Even though it's bigger than her small body, she's trying to pull her garbage bin back towards the building but it's fallen over and now she's just kicking it again and again like it's the garbage bin's fault.

'Eh,' my dad is yelling down at her, 'don't worry Esther, I'll send Michael down to help you,' but Esther's not listening. She's got the bottom of the garbage can now and she's dragging it back with its wheels like it's some naughty child.

'Don't need help,' she yells, 'I got it now.'

And we all sit back on the fold-out chairs so she doesn't see us laughing. Poppy sits there, hands over his pot belly almost screaming with laughter; that's the safety net of oldness, you can do whatever you want and people just shrug and put up with you.

Dad's not much of a laugher but he's smiling, as always. He's got those big teeth and the sideways grin like Dom.

Mum used to laugh a lot but she doesn't much now. She doesn't laugh hardly at all really. She just sits there with her pale blank face. She laughs sometimes and then I watch her suck it back in, deep into her belly, where it gets stuck and doesn't come back out again.

Aunty Leena, she's got a laugh that's totally infectious. She says it's her job to make me laugh now and most of the time she's the only one that does. And Sam, you just know they're related because he tips his head back in the same way as Aunty Leena and laughs, his whole body shaking, like he just doesn't care who's watching.

Dom's not here to laugh at Esther with us anymore but he is always laughing in my dreams, always finding the world a very funny place.

Shadi, his cousin and his other cousin

This time when we go to the pool we take Shadi's two cousins with us – just in case. Shadi isn't aggressive at all. He has like zero bashing experience. That's what his cousins are for. They are bigger than him and better at looking mean. Shadi looks too much like his mother mated with Roger Rabbit to be threatening.

We settle in our usual spot underneath the trees and Shadi's cousins take off their shirts so they're sitting there, all rippling six-pack flesh.

Shadi and I just look at each other and I know what he's thinking and he knows what I'm thinking. We have to get away from these two before girls start making comparisons between us and them and it all gets too embarrassing.

We cannon-bomb into the water at the deep end of the pool. Shadi's face comes up all wobbly and we look over to his cousins to make sure they're still there. Still there alright and they're already talking to girls...Mo's friends and Mo is sitting there, on the outside of their giggling circle just nodding.

I decide to play it cool, ducking my head under the water and swimming a few more laps like I don't even notice she's there. I'm still playing it cool, just watching the bubbles surrounding my arms come up to the surface and pop when Shadi swims over and almost drowns me with excitement. 'Check it out,' he's saying a bit too loud and when I look over to what he's looking at, I see the bikini-top floating on the surface of the water.

Shadi's looking from side to side and so am I at this point, trying to determine where it came from, until we see her, this super blond frail-looking thing, shrinking in the corner of the pool, her arms wrapped tightly over her bare chest looking like she's going to cry.

Then Shadi is yelling, 'Don't worry, don't worry,' loudly over to her, drawing the attention you know she doesn't want, and then he's grabbing the bikini-top and swimming it over to her like he's found her lost dog.

She grabs it with her pinky, so her arms don't leave her chest and turns herself back to the corner of the pool where she puts it back on faster than you can blink. When she turns around again she bursts into tears, like loud howling kind of tears and Shadi goes into a kindness panic. He's saying, 'It's fine, it's cool,' over and over again and then he's got his arm around her and he's leading her out of the pool and over to the trees where his cousins are sitting.

I swim around the pool a little bit more, keeping my head out of the water, watching them. I'm thinking, you fool, last thing I'd be doing with a girl is taking her over near your cousins to be snapped up.

I swim another lap, like I'm not paying attention and I sneak a glance at what Mo's doing. She's lying on the grass with her head looking straight up to the sky, ignoring everyone else. That girl is so beautiful it makes me want to kill myself.

Then I catch sight of something even more amazing. Shadi, 'the last man on earth'.

The type of guy that makes girls say:

Not for a million dollars.

Not for a kiss from Robert Pattinson.

Not for all the clothes at Sportsgirl.

He's sitting there with his arm around this girl and she's smiling up at him through her freckles like *he is* the only man in the world. Shadi's cousin and his other cousin are noticing it too and all the boys are sitting there grinning like it's Christmas.

Granville Servo

Sometimes, on Saturday mornings we work at Shadi's parent's petrol station in Granville. It's the only place on the street that's not selling food or God. It's squashed into the space between the Ethiopian Jehovah's Witnesses and one of the charcoal chicken places. Shadi likes to put on the radio in the shop and crank up the volume just so people know we're there.

On. these mornings Shadi always brings a bag of roasted pumpkin seeds. He passes me a handful and we practise splitting them perfectly between our front teeth and poking the seed out with our tongues. When Mohammed comes, he'll show us how it's done.

Most of the time I either end up eating the whole

thing or spitting it out in a big mess on the pavement. Shadi places another seed in his mouth, chokes and spits out the sharp fragments of a shell. I just laugh and squint at the sun behind Shadi's head.

When Mohammed comes he smiles and nods at us. He doesn't need to make any demands; he just goes and people follow him. He's like my brother, walking in his too-low jeans, walking like he owns the place. He looks ten-feet tall, even if he's really only five-five. He runs his hand over his dark, shaved head and gets those heavy keys out, opens up the door and sits on his stool behind the counter. That's where he'll stay most of the time, while Shadi and I fuss around the place.

The morning goes like this: after all the lights are turned on, the shelves stacked, the fridges humming, the three of us go outside and lean against the front wall like we're gangsters from *The Fast and The Furious*, then we pass around the packet of pumpkin seeds and get to practising while we wait for customers to appear.

Not many people are out this early on a Saturday morning. It's too early for anyone except the nannas pushing trolleys loaded with fruit and digestive biscuits and young men looking hazy from the night before. Shadi keeps going on and on about that blond girl, Sal, he rescued at the pool. Mohammed nods and yells 'Yalla!' at his mate across the road who's come out of his chicken shop to get the morning sun too.

I watch the sun tear over the *Jesus Saves* sign and listen to my stomach grumble. This close to Easter I'm always thinking of chocolate but Granville makes me think of chicken too. Chocolate. Chicken. Pumpkin seeds. Somewhere down the road, underneath the chimneys spilling the smell of roasting chicken there is the sound of some preacher's low voice going on and on and on and a bunch of people yellin' *Amen!*

Sounds

In the neighbourhood there are all sorts of sounds. At night is when you can really hear things if you're still and you listen hard. Sometimes on Friday nights there is the sound of the Eels kicking off at the stadium, you can even hear it; the kick, the ball flying through the air, the crowd waiting to scream. But most times it's other things like someone in the next apartment building practising recorder or someone stopping too fast at a stop sign.

Before, I used to listen for the sound of Dom coming home but I haven't got that to listen for anymore. Now there is the sound of my father walking back and forth and up and down the hallway of our apartment. Sometimes I don't think my dad is doing as well as he wants us to think.

I'm learning new things about people all the time.

Walking Instead

Today, Shadi and me are going to meet Sal and Mo at the pool. It's getting cooler and there won't be too much time left for pools soon. I can hear him knocking on the door long before I can get up off the couch and let him in. It's one of those days when things move really slowly, like so slowly that I'm sitting there on the couch and I know that someone's knocking and I know that it must be Shadi but I can't get up anyway.

When I do get to the door Shadi is standing there and he's looking at me like *what happened to you?*

'You alright?' he says, looking at me, just standing like I'm stuck or something.

'Yeh, fine.'

'Where's your swimmers?'

I look down. I'm wearing my thick old winter jeans and I can't remember why I put them on.

'Oh, I don't know.'

Shadi stands there leaning against the door and adjusts his swim trunks so that more of his big fat belly is on the inside of his pants than the outside. 'Maybe we skip the pool today? Maybe we just hang out together? We could go have a walk or talk or not talk or you could just continue standing there looking like crap or whatever, you know, you need to do or anything.'

'Yeh,' I say. That's all I can say but it's still like a big weight off my shoulders. I can't answer that question, *how are you feeling?* any more. It makes me nervous, the way everyone asks it all the time like I'm never coming up with the right answer.

Shadi puts his arm around my shoulder and leads me out of the apartment. We walk down the stairs. We walk out of the building. We walk onto the street and keep on going.

Sometimes I think Shadi is dumb but he's not. He knows that sometimes you just need to walk in silence because you're stuck thinking about the before and after and it's too hard to be thinking about anything else.

Hooters and Horses

Sunday afternoons, Poppy goes to the Rosehill Bowling Club. Sometimes Shadi and I go along. Dad likes it that we go with Poppy, he thinks we'll keep him out of trouble. But Shadi and I, we go precisely for the trouble *and* because the bowling club is next to Hooters *and* because Poppy buys us unlimited hot chips.

Poppy wipes the counter and sets the form guide down in front of the three of us. Then Poppy goes into his teacher's mode. He explains the weather conditions on the track, that some horses are better in wet or in dry weather, that the odds on one horse are now really good because he's got a new trainer from Hong Kong, that his mate Angelo gave him privileged information that will surely lead to some big money. Poppy explains how he chooses his horse and then we get to pick out horses we would bet on if we were allowed to. Shadi and I, we always go for the ones with the most ridiculous-sounding names. Shadi picks Shakira Shake and I pick Million Dollar Mama.

After Poppy puts his betting forms in, no one is allowed to talk, at least not to Poppy, he gets himself glued to the little screens in the corner, like the whole world might fall in if he stops watching. His body freezes up like he's some kind of fat, balding statue. So me and Shadi get Cokes from the vending machines on the lawn and hang over the fence trying to get a look at the Hooters girls. They must be on to guys like us because they've got all these plants and decorations and things in their windows so you can't see so well from the outside. But, if you look long enough, there's always something – a bit of leg, some woman flipping her hair back.

Sometimes, if we're really bored, we play a game of bowls. We're always the youngest ones there playing but the old people in their wide-brimmed hats and their medical-coat outfits move aside for us.

Shadi places the little white ball at the end of our playing strip and we begin to go at it. We don't play this game nice and slow, stopping to have a chat, considering our moves. We go at it as fast as we can, hurling the balls down the lawn one after the other, so that we finish our games in ten minutes flat: not much skill, not much precision, me and Shadi, but it's fun.

By the time the old players are looking frustrated out

of their brains watching me and Shadi play, Poppy comes out onto the court with two gigantic bowls of hot chips and we know he's won. The three of us sit there on the benches eating and Poppy exclaims, '$300! Could have got more if your mother let me take more money.'

Me and Shadi grin at him through mouths stuffed with chips and I say, 'Ah well. That's enough for today,' like Dad would say, knowing if we don't grab him and leave he'd be perfectly happy to sit on the poker machines and spend all afternoon blowing that $300 he's got now. So I get up and shove as many chips in my mouth as I can at one time and Shadi does too. 'Come on,' I say smiling a chippy smile and me and Shadi walk him out the door before he gets a chance to protest.

We walk him home, on past Hooters, catching a glimpse of orange short-shorts through the window.

Aunty Leena says it's good for me

She says I wear worry on my face too much, though I never seem to notice it. But taking care of other people you don't have time for so much worry so sometimes Aunty Leena brings over Sam and tells me to take care of him for the day. I take him up to Lake Parramatta. The start of autumn and everything is beginning to go yellow and brown. Leaves are falling everywhere. We go searching for fish in the places other people don't go like near the long grasses on the north-western side of the lake. I grab Sam's hand and pull him up over the slippery flat rocks. When we reach the clearing we toss our bodies down on dry patches of dirt and throw rocks into the water for a while before we get to the fishing. I am trying to show Sam, what Dom showed me once, how you can skip flat stones across water so that they land somewhere far on the other side of the lake. Sam picks up rocks all over the place, the wrong type of rocks that aren't flat enough to skip and throws them bang up into the sky so that they come down and land in big plops in the water.

Sam talks and talks and I just let him go off. Aunty Leena says this is how you take care of people by just listening to whatever they have to say. Sam talks about all the kids in his class like they're so famous I should know exactly who they are, then he goes into his question-asking thing: 'What's your favourite colour? Where'd you learn to skip rocks? If you were a car what kind of car would you be?'

'Easy,' I say, 'a Pontiac Trans Am.'

But Sam's not listening, he's farting off more questions before I can even think of the answers. I keep nodding my head as Sam talks. He's got those puffy cheeks and fat eyelashes like Aunty Leena that always make him look like he's super-excited. Later, I'll get him hot chips at the lake shop. I finger the coins in my pocket.

Poppy's Stories

Poppy, he loves telling stories. He sits there on his chair on the lawn and he leans forward, his legs wide open and his arms on his knees, his belly hanging over his too-tight polyester pants. He's so close to me sitting on my chair that I can see the red veins on his nose and I know it's going to be a good story.

He tells me the story of the time when a fourteen-year-old Dom stole a six pack he found inside his room at the home. 'I knew it was him. Obvious you know? He must have stuck it in his school bag when he went to the bathroom, like I wouldn't notice six cans missing. I was going to talk to him about it but before I could, I found him passed out in the park across the road a couple of hours later.'

'Your mum always thought the sun and the moon and the stars shined out his arse. That boy was trouble. That's why I miss him so much.' Poppy leans in closer so I can feel his beer breath on my cheek and says 'It's alright to miss him you know.'

McDonald's is the Centre of the Universe

Because we can't get into One World Bar, because they won't let us go dancing at The Roxy, because the cafés are filled with too-old people, because the parks are filled with dodgy strangers, because we've already seen all the movies at Greater Union and Westfield is shut at night, because of all of this, the McDonald's parking lot is the centre of our night-time universe, at least for now.

Everyone that has a car, or knows someone who does, parks and sits there spilling out their windows. This evening we've been lucky enough to get Shadi's cousin's Commodore. Shadi gave his cousin the twenty dollars his mother gives him every week (behind his father's back), to let us and Mo and Shadi's girl, Sal from the pool, sit in it while he goes off to meet his mates at the movies.

Since Shadi's cousin has guaranteed that we will both lose our balls if we sit on his newly reconditioned leather seats with McDonald's hamburgers, the four of us are standing outside the car eating. I had a new haircut and brought Mo some flowers I nicked from the front of our apartment building. Shadi's got a new shirt on. I think we're doing pretty well.

We eat and watch two guys break-dancing on the concrete and the girls let out a little squeal and get closer to us each time they jump head first onto the ground and spin.

Now that I've got through my nervousness, I'm completely exhausted. I listen to what Mo has to say about all sorts of things I don't know nothing about. She tells me about her school, her father's fruit shop, the family trips back to Egypt every summer. Mo doesn't like *The Fast and The Furious* or video games or the Parramatta Eels. She likes books about travel and studying French. She likes the Twilight movies. She likes Robert Pattinson. She likes to talk and talk. She speaks without drawing breath so that I lose the ability to follow along until she says, 'Michael, are you listening to me?' like Mum used to say. I put my arm around her and we lean against the iridescent green of that car.

She smiles that amazing smile and says, 'I'm cold,' and I don't have anything to give her so we climb into the front seat of the car and sit shoved up against each other. In the back seat Shadi (Shadi!) is making out with Sal, I can see Mo watching them through the rear-view mirror so I decide to make my move. I put my hand on her thigh and lean in.

She leans back and says, 'Nah, time to go home,' then she's silent for the first time in the evening and we both stare out into the parking lot, watching everyone in the McDonald's universe coming and going.

Above

Some days I go hang out with Mo in her parent's fruit shop. At these times, she wears loose-hanging cargo pants and old faded shirts with *Nike* or *Pepsi* logos across the front. I help her move boxes of oranges and apples to the displays at the front. She talks and we run our hands through the barrels of vegetables and fruit, picking out things that have gone too soft for the bargain baskets.

Mo doesn't hold back from asking about anything. I am passing her cucumbers that are beginning to go wrinkly when she asks me, 'So how exactly did your brother die? Was it in the car or did it happen after?'

'His head hit the inside of the car really hard, when it was spinning. He just didn't wake up again.' I pretend to get distracted from the conversation by grabbing at an off-coloured peach, smelling it, turning it around in my hands.

'Huh. Just like that and he's gone.'

'Yep.' *Just like that, he's driving and then he's dead.* But I don't say it, not out loud. I put the peach back and pick up another. I am hoping she won't ask me any more questions and she doesn't. She gets stuck staring at a bunch of grapes that have fallen to the ground. I have thought about it too, many times, the fact that someone can be there and then not there so quickly. There. Not there. It's a difficult thing to get your head around. It's not as simple as it sounds.

Mo's parents and her brothers take the truck to the markets in the early mornings to get the good stuff and in the afternoons to get what's left over and cheap. While they're gone, we sneak out back to the stairs that lead to their apartment above the shop.

At these times Mo actually stops talking for a while and we can knock about in silence, just being comfortable, being together. Mo makes me coffee from a little Turkish coffee pot she puts on the stove and we drink it with yellow biscuits.

The whole place smells like overripe fruit, the same smell that Mo has when she's standing next me.

'Must be hard,' she says all of a sudden, chewing into a bit of biscuit and I know she's thinking about the there and the not there thing again.

'You get used to it,' I say and end the conversation right there. 'You have like a million stuffed animals on your bed.'

'Yeh, I know,' she says turning around to her bedroom door, open behind the kitchen.

I've told her a lot but I don't want to tell her any more. I don't want to explain exactly what happened or the dreams I have at night of cars spinning through the sky. People are there and then they're not there, but right now we're above her parent's fruit shop. We're here.

Night Swimming

A new thing Shadi and I have just discovered – there are other places to go at night besides McDonald's, like the swimming pool where we go during the day but at night-time it's completely different. It's too cold at night to be there really but I don't think anyone cares. It's ours.

This night, Shadi and I take Sal and Mo through the hole in the back of the chain-link fence. I pull back the fence at the corner where I cut it straight with a pair of pliers from my dad's shop last time we were here. You can't even see the cut. With a bit of effort I can pull it back and forth just like that, like opening a tin can and no one even notices.

Mo goes in first with no effort at all and then stands

there on the other side watching the three of us scratching ourselves against the fence and falling over our feet. At night-time the place is quiet, even with all the noise of the streets around it. It's like arriving in another universe. Sal and Mo sit on the edge of the pool with their feet in, talking quietly. Shadi too, unlike Shadi, is quiet. He takes off his shirt, slips into the water at the deep end of the pool and swims towards the shallow end where the girls are. I stand underneath one of the trees and watch Shadi's neon green swim trunks dip in and out of the pool water. When he reaches Sal she pulls her dress off her head so that she's sitting there at the edge of the pool in her swimmers. She puts her arms on his shoulders and he puts his hands on her hips and pulls her slowly into the pool where they swim off together to the other side. It's a different kind of Shadi when he's with Sal.

I'm trying to get myself together before I go over to Mo. She's so beautiful it makes me feel like I'm exploding with wanting her. She's looking off into the distance of the street, away from me. The moon has broken all over her head and she looks like she's glowing there in the yellow dress she's wearing.

I take my shirt off and sit beside her in my swim shorts. She kicks her legs slowly around in the water and so do I. Sometimes our legs are touching. Sometimes not. This place makes everyone quiet. I kiss the freckles on her shoulder and ask, 'So what are you thinking?'

Mo puts her hand on my knee and laughs into the water. 'That's my question. That's what I ask you. But you always change the subject.'

'Well I thought maybe if I ask you first you'll stop asking me.' In the water, our legs and our feet look bent backward and out of shape. In the bits of light from the street and the moon it looks like our feet are disappearing and regrowing again.

'I'm thinking, I forgot to put my swimmers on.'

'Doesn't matter. We can just sit here anyway.' And we do until the moment Mo pushes herself into the water in that yellow dress and swims across to the other side of the pool. She's amazing. She looks like a stream of yellow paint just floating there. I jump in and swim towards her until I meet her in the corner of the pool. Her dress floats up around me and the fabric gets all caught around my legs like it's pulling me in and I am, I'm totally pulled in, leaning against her in the corner, her lips are like warm rubber and I've got a bunch of her wet hair in my right hand and suddenly she says 'fuck' and it takes me a while to realise what she's talking about as she pushes me away from her and I realise that it's not her yellow dress glowing. All the lights around the pool have been turned on and then from somewhere, an alarm.

Assembly

First day back after the Easter holidays and Tom, as usual, has his legs wide open so that he can slouch down at the back of the assembly and draw a dick on his chair. There is nothing else to do at assemblies but draw dicks on chairs or call each other gay. I am watching him draw in the second ball when Mr Smith comes up behind him and says, 'What's the matter you don't have one yourself?' And then Tom and the chair are gone and all the boys are slumped over trying not to laugh too loud.

When Mr Alloshi walks up to the stage one thousand boys straighten themselves up in their chairs momentarily. That fat old Mr Alloshi, we sit there watching as he begins to turn red from the bottom of his neck all the way up to his big round face. It's funny how angry this man can get just by watching boys fidgeting; desperately funny, miserably funny. We sit there and wait for him to burst, hot and suffocated by the airless auditorium and each other's BO.

Mr Alloshi gets up and lectures everyone about the term ahead. He is saying something about 'responsibility, *yadah, yadah*, hard, work, *yadah, yadah*.' I'm singing something by The Black Eyed Peas in my head and Shadi looks like he must be doing the same the way his head is bobbing up and down.

When the lecture is over we all stand up and file out. I catch Shadi, finally, and we squeeze through the doors together and out into the big hot of the yard.

'I still think Mo has bigger balls than any of us,' he says for like the fourteen millionth time since what she did that night at the pool.

Gifts

Dom's friends ring the intercom four times. When I open the door David and Yousef are standing there with plates of pancakes, Mark's got a wobbly tower of red jelly and James has a bowl of cream in one hand and a card in the other. They all look as if they've scrubbed themselves down and are ready to be on their best behaviour.

'Bro!' Mark says, stepping forward. He tucks the jelly under one arm and shakes my hand with the other. It's been almost four months since I saw him at the funeral.

'Nice jelly.' It's getting squished under his armpit and I'm waiting for the whole thing to explode and fall all over the white tiles of the hallway.

'I made it myself,' he says pulling it out of his armpit.

'From a packet.'

The boys all shove their way through the door as politely as they can. They kiss my mother on the cheek and give her plates of food and the whip-cream bowl and the card.

My father stands beside my mother in the living room like they're accepting important company and not these guys they've seen a thousand times over making a mess of their living-room floor.

My father holds up the bowl of cream and stares at it like he's worried there might be something wrong with it. 'Whip cream?'

'For the pancakes and the jelly. Everything tastes better with cream,' Yousef says and all the boys laugh like it's some kind of private secret.

'Right, right. Dom always made pancakes too.'

'I know. He taught us how to make them.'

Dad looks all awkward again. 'Thanks for coming over.' He says. Why don't you boys sit down and talk with Michael. We'll get you some drinks.'

The guys sprawl out on the couches and the chairs. I missed Dom's boys. The way they completely take up every space they're in, even if it's outside. James beats his fist against the inside of his other hand. Yousef puts his arms behind his head and lays back on the couch. David sits on my left and Mark sits on my right and puts his hand over my shoulder like we're real good mates.

They've gone browner since I saw them last and their shoulders have become more square so that they each look like a solid box. David rubs the top of my head hard with his knuckles and asks me about girls.

I play it cool. I say 'Yeh, maybe…I got someone.'

The boys are like, 'Bro,' and they each give me a headlock or hit me in the arm or give me a high five. I pull Mo's Facebook picture up on my phone and they each have a good look at it and hit me again.

'Awesome,' Mark says, 'she looks like that Puerto Rican chick in the first *Fast and The Furious.*'

I nod my head and put the phone back into my pocket and stretch myself out on the couch. David is telling me about all the things they've seen in the summer driving over to Bondi, like one of the teachers in a bikini and hairy-backed Adam Poulos with two good-looking girls, who were probably related to him, but still, and Swedish women sunbathing with no tops on.

Every one of them boys has seen something great there and they tell me they'll take me too, maybe next weekend. I can share the middle in the front of David's car, like I used to next to Dom and we can all drive East like we did before. Dom's boys say they got my back on anything I need and it makes me feel good.

I leave them for a minute to go into the kitchen and see where the drinks and the pancakes and the jelly and the cream got to. Mum and Dad are sitting at the kitchen table. Dad's eating a bowl of jelly and staring off into space and Mum's crying without sound. They've got that card the boys bought in front of them. I lean over behind them and I can see that the boys have all written long messages there.

Bach

Aunty Leena is dragging Sam, a massive picnic basket, two blankets and a foldout chair up the hill in Parramatta Park. She splits open the crowds of people and we follow her – me, Dad, Mum and Mo. This thing isn't what I thought it might be with everyone looking all proper like the time the school took us to the Opera House. The park is full of women in their short-shorts and tight jeans and men with too-big bellies.

Aunty Leena lays down her blankets and picnic baskets and me and Mo set up the pink towels she brought from her house and the fruit salad her mum made. We sit ourselves among all the other hot bodies.

'There now,' Aunty Leena says, waving to a spot for

Poppy and Mum and Dad to sit down. 'I guess we just wait for the music.'

Aunty Leena is more Tupac than Bach so it was a bit strange when she wanted to drag everyone along to a classical concert but Dad thought it would be a good idea to do something as a family and Poppy wanted to meet Mo. I wasn't sure if I wanted Mo to meet him but he promised he'd be on his best behaviour.

'Have you ever heard of Bach?' Poppy is saying to Mo, leaning over her, too close, so I know he's trying to get a good long look.

'Yeh,' Mo leans forward, brushes all her thick curls over her shoulder and smiles through pink lip gloss, 'guy with a wig.'

And Poppy smiles back at her, his red cheeks puffing out and I know he likes her because she's cheeky like him. I look out at the crowd and wonder how many of them actually know any more than we know. I watch Dad put his hand over Mum's. After the accident he stopped planting big sloppy kisses on her forehead and chin. Now this is the way they touch, softly, like Mum might fall apart if he does it any other way. Watching Mum and Dad together like this makes me feel heavy inside. I look at Aunty Leena and she winks at me and some of the heaviness lifts.

The Bach stuff begins when a couple of dozen men and women come out on the stage dressed in black; black suits, black ties, black dresses like they should be at a funeral, not here in the park in autumn.

The guy with a stick comes out and bows and the music begins. Aunty Leena passes me a bottle of grape juice and I take a sip and pass it to Mo. Her eyebrows are all close together and her big brown eyes are staring real hard at the stage and I can tell that she's concentrating. She takes my hand and puts it on the grass, 'Feel that,' the music is pumping out from the stage and spreading underground like a maze of pipes. Mo's touching the ground and smiling and then Sam's doing it too, giggling at the vibrating grass.

Sam starts making noises like the Transformers he likes to watch on TV, 'Bzzz, bzzz', and Mo joins him. I watch them and I wish that I could lay Mo down right here on the ground and touch her in all sorts of places.

They stop when the crowd falls more silent and you know the music is building up to something big. Even Sam stops playing and listens. For a moment I feel like I am walking into the music, like I understand it. Then just like that I'm nowhere near the music again.

When the music stops and the people on stage are getting themselves together for the next song, it begins to rain lightly. People start to get up and move so that there's a better line of view to the stage. I look at my family. Sam is clapping his hands to the beat of something going on inside his own head.

I know we're not going anywhere so I don't move

and Mo doesn't move either. We sit on the grass so long listening to that music that the wet goes through the towel and into my underwear, listening to stuff with no words.

Coke

Mornings. I walk down the highway past the old weatherboard houses just stewing there, their screen doors open, hanging off their rusted hinges, slamming in the breeze of an almost winter morning. Everyone walks past me on their way to school. They're walking faster than I walk, slamming their arms into each other's sides, like there just ain't enough space in all the world.

Some kid yells out, 'Your Aunty Leena's a MILF,' as he walks by slapping the roughness of his two-dollar-shop backpack against the back of my arm.

I steer myself into the front gates of the Coke factory and let its crisscrossed wires hold me there. This is where we used to come, Dom and me. We'd stand here on our way to school just staring through the fence, imagining the mountains of sugar laying just beyond our reach. He'd start singing the Coke song, 'Open up, open up some happiness,' in his loud off-key way. Dom had big dreams of breaking in one day, of scaling the walls of its giant rectangular surfaces and diving into a sea of Coke.

I can hear the first morning bell ringing in the distance and I know that it's my cue to keep on walking, but I don't. I get distracted by the factory's hum and the neat rows of Coke machines glinting in the morning sun and I stand there some more until I can feel him, like he's here. Then I picture him somewhere inside those big grey buildings, floating in the bubbling brown liquid, Coke bleeding through his thick hair.

Bread-Shop Man

Hey,' he says in his croaky voice as me and Mo walk towards Bread-Shop Man sitting on his milk crate outside his shop. He always looks like he has just come up for air, like he might have accidently put himself in his red brick oven.

The Bread-Shop Man gets up and goes to stand in between his oven and his counter again. 'Hey, Hey,' he says gesturing to the two types of bread he makes here in his oven. I don't know what the difference between his two types of bread is but I know that one tastes like pancakes and the other one doesn't. I point to one of the giant round disks of brown spotted bread sitting in neat rows just outside his oven. He brings it over to the counter with his giant spatula and wraps it in a piece of white butcher's paper.

'Hot. Hot,' he says as he passes the package over to us, releasing it from his hard red hands. 'Thanks,' I say and hand over a few coins. This place is too hard to take for more than a few minutes at a time. Even this time of year when things are cooling down.

Mo and I go and sit on the tombstones in the park across the road and eat our pancake bread in the last bits of autumn sun. From there we can see Bread-Shop Man coming out from the shop to sit on his milk crate again. He stares off down the street just watching, watching. He unties the thick knot of curly black hair he keeps in a ponytail and lets his hair fall every which way. Then he ties it back up again and keeps on looking down the road, arms folded across his chest, just watching.

Toilets

That second term back, I spend a lot of time in the toilet. Mrs Oliver keeps looking at me in homeroom and says, 'What? Again?' and then later, 'Is there something wrong with you Michael? Something you might want to talk about?'

'Nah, just gotta go,' but I don't really. I just want some time away from everyone. I want to sit in there, behind the cubicle door, among the whitewashed tiles and the smells of bleach, in this early morning time before it begins to really smell like boys. I close the door and put my iPod on. I listen to the Gorillaz or the Black Eyed Peas.

I know that there is stuff going on inside me, stuff I can't put words to, so I just sit there feeling the music, feeling like I'm closing in on myself.

Above and Below

Above and below: these are two very different spaces. Looking out the window from Mo's place above the shop, below is a bunch of grey old buildings, some vacant, some not. These buildings are filled with little pastry shops and foods labelled in the languages of other countries. The whole street looks dusty like it isn't being used, there is the odd lady with a shopping bag and kids just wandering, nowhere to go.

But inside, in this space above the whole world, I'm sitting on the sofa that smells like squashed grapes with Mo's hand tucked up under mine. 'Still can't believe it. Imagine what that security guard thought when he showed up. This yellow wet girl running towards him. I don't think any of us would have got back through the fence if you hadn't done that.'

'I think he actually believed me for a second there when I told him I'd gotten lost. Or maybe he just thought I was a crazy or something. When I ran through the gate he'd opened, it took him like five whole minutes to start running after me. He didn't have a chance.'

Everything she does is amazing. I want to peel her clothes back as if I'm ripping the skin off an orange. I don't look at her because I can't. I look at the wall and I squeeze her hand and I smile as she tells me the story.

'Look at me,' she says and I do but I'm feeling nervous. I'm trying really hard to look into her big brown eyes and not look down at her boobs.

'Do you want to kiss me?' she asks, moving over closer.

'Yeh,' I say and then 'Yes, yes I do,' in case the first time wasn't convincing enough and then she's closer to me, like right up to my face and her lips are touching mine. I'm kissing her and trying to work out what to do with my arms. I put them on her hips and move in so that I can feel her hip bones there pressing against her jeans.

I move one of my sweaty hands up her shirt and try to work my fingers into the front of her bra. She lets my fingers stop there, just for a moment before she pulls away again, to the other side of the couch, wiping her mouth with the back of her sleeve. She sits there and smiles that amazing smile. 'I think we'd better go down below to the shop. My dad'll wonder where we are.'

And then, just like that, we're moving downstairs again when all I want is to be alone with her in that space above this world.

Looking For God

Last time, they were Mormons, before that Baptists from Southern Africa, around Christmas time it's always the Salvos. Poppy can't get the ones who dress like it's 1880 to talk to him but he likes the women's little white caps. The rabbi with the red beard always says hello on his way down the street and so does the man in the white dress with the big wooden beads he says he keeps his worries in. Poppy says Parramatta is the home of God because we've got all types of godly people here.

They talk to Poppy because he doesn't tell them to go away like everyone else does. He actually likes talking to them. Or, mostly, he just likes to ask them really hard questions they can never answer and then to watch them looking uncomfortable.

Today, I think the woman is from the Korean Catholic Church. When I get to the home they are sitting in the plastic chairs on the lawn and Poppy keeps interrupting whatever she's saying with 'But,' and then he launches into some big long speech until this woman, she doesn't even try anymore. She just sits there with her tight bun in her hair and her flower dress, her lips smacked together in a little heart. Poppy sips his beer and offers the woman one and she says no and plays with her hands in her lap.

'Hi,' I say. I want to get in that I'm there before Poppy starts up again. It takes Poppy a minute to register I'm there even though I'm right in front of him.

'Aye' he says, 'sit down' and I plop down on one of the chairs next to the woman, who is looking like she's trying real hard to come up with the next thing to say.

'Now this one,' Poppy says, pointing at me, 'he lost his brother, how do you explain that?' and the word *explain* comes out all awkward sounding and I look at him and he's got a look like Mum gets these days and I realise that he really wants the answer, like God has really made him angry and sad all at the same time and this makes my heart jump up in my chest.

I look at the woman and I ask her, 'but how can someone be there one day and then not the next?' Her eyebrows go up in her forehead and she plays with her hands in her lap.

Poppy takes a deep breath and stares into his beer can, 'Everyone needs answers sometimes.'

119

Essential Information

I walk down to the park where my brother buried his magazines, next to the old convict tombstones, across the road from the house with 'Go the Eels' spray-painted on its tin roof. I've got the garden spade Poppy uses to plant herbs on our balcony.

I've got sex in my head. There is sex between me and Mo but we're not actually having any sex. Dom would know what I mean. He knew about things like girls and sex. Sometimes I think it made him a bit retarded because he couldn't think about anything else. My brother, he liked girls more madly than I've ever seen anyone like girls. It was like he knew, always, what direction you could find them in.

So when I get to the park I start digging. It doesn't take long. The old plastic Coles bags he stored the magazines in are only a foot deep. I take the bag and go sit underneath one of the trees where no one else will ever come and I spread the pile out before me. There are two old *Playboys* my brother bought at a second-hand shop and three copies of *Hustler* his friends gave him for his sixteenth birthday.

I look at the images of all these women lying there and I don't really think that any of them look anything like Mo would if she took off all her clothes. None of the articles are really all that useful. I find out that Miss January likes a man who listens, that there's a lip-gloss that changes colour when women are in the mood, that there are restaurants in Japan that serve raw fish on a woman's naked body and you can learn about giving women orgasms from the Chinese. I stare at the women wearing bras with no undies or undies with no bras.

Out There

Mr Alloshi is in one long continual state of explosion. The hair he has left is sticking up in a shock of grey like there's too much electricity in the room and his eyes are bugging out of their deep blue sockets. He's sitting there with his stomach bulging out of his pants and his arms crossed over like he's trying to push his middle bits back in.

In his right hand he holds up a stamp that says SUSPENDED in big red letters on the side. He stamps it everywhere on the papers that lie on his desk. I'm sitting there waiting for him to lunge forward and stamp it on my forehead just to make sure I get the point.

'But I wasn't skipping school. I was just in the toilet,' I say to him again.

His face turns even redder and he presses his lips forward and outward like his head might explode, 'You failed to show up to any classes after recess. That's skipping class, I don't care where you were. If you have to spend that long in the toilet then you need a medical certificate.'

'But...' I begin to say but he holds his stamp out again like a threat until I decide to swallow the rest of my words.

Then he begins his lecture again, 'You kids don't understand. There's a whole world out there where you have to obey the rules. You get a job, you're expected to show up. If you don't learn that in here, you'll never cope out there.'

I want to say something again but I bite my lip. No point. This man, he doesn't even know what *out there* is like.

Riots

A riot in Harris Park. We saw it on the TV. Shadi and I are stoked. We were too young for Cronulla but now we've got one of our own and we can walk there. Shadi's just about pissing his pants.

When we arrive, there's nothing much though. Harris Park is like the smallest neighbourhood ever. They've only really got a big roundabout, four streets leading off it and a small strip of shops on each one. This afternoon there's more happening on that roundabout than I've ever seen but it still isn't much. There's like thirty police standing in four equal rows so they make a square around the roundabout. The police are all wearing jackets that say RIOT in big letters, like a promise they aren't keeping.

On top of the roundabout there's about forty Indian guys. They're all young. All dressed in jeans and hoodies and beanies and t-shirts with the names of American universities. They don't look so scary. They've got their arms up and every now and then someone shouts 'Yeh!' at the guy in the middle who I can't understand because he's speaking some other language but you can tell he's giving this huge speech and that everyone's really interested.

Shadi and I stand back behind the orange streamers with all the people who are watching in front of the hairdressers. Me and Shadi lean up against the glass wall and wait for the action to happen on the roundabout but the action is heaps better on the sidelines. The police have shut down the shops so that everyone who's supposed to be working is standing around. The lady who usually sells the eggs in big trays at the Indian grocer is saying, 'It's not a riot. It is a protest. This is important for a democracy. This is how we do things in India.' She folds her arms over her apron and nods towards the crowd of young Indian men on the roundabout.

The man who sells olives at the Lebanese grocer laughs like she has said the funniest thing but you can tell he doesn't think she's funny at all because his laugh comes out all fake-sounding. 'Last night from my apartment above my shop, I watched them drag this Lebanese boy out of his car and beat him in the gutter. What for? For nothing. This is not a protest thing to do.'

'Just one boy?' the woman says much louder than she said anything before and the crowd that's gathered around stop looking at the shouting guys on the roundabout and turn to look at these two.

The guy next to Shadi holds out an open packet of chips towards both of us and it's like everyone is settling in to watch the fight scene in a movie.

Another guy turns to the Lebanese grocer and says, 'that's nothing, these Indian students, they get bashed by those Lebanese boys every time they walk back from the train station.'

'Not true,' someone else says.

'Wouldn't matter where they came from. They're skinny and they've always got money and they're a real easy target.'

'My cousin...'

'Your cousin, your cousin. Shut up.'

Shadi whispers in my ear, 'This is like The Eels vs The Bulldogs.'

But I'm thinking it's more like that time when all those Sudanese kids showed up in class because their country fell apart or something and no one could work out how you're supposed to be friendly.

'I couldn't give a shit where any of you come from,' another guy says. 'I just want to get back to my shop.'

Mo Knows

Mo knows everything. She's like Aunty Leena and how my mum used to be before she went quiet. This afternoon we are lying on the grass. It's too cold really this time of year but the afternoon sun has at least made the ice on the grass melt. And I'm lying here, just relaxing, looking at the clouds, trying to empty my head of anything that isn't good.

Mo, she won't sit still. She's wandering all around the place. I roll over on my side and watch her in the distance running her hands along the sandy walls of the old mental hospital. She's been looking at those walls all morning, like they're gonna tell her a story or something.

Now, she's just standing there, staring up at the clock that doesn't work. I watch her turn her head slowly and take the whole building in, like she's some kind of scientist studying it real seriously with her arms folded across her chest. I like it here, even if I can't get Mo to lie down still on the grass with me. It's quiet and private as if you're in a whole other time.

She's back again eventually. She sits down beside me on the grass and puts her hand through my hair but she's not looking at me at all. She's still looking at the building.

'It's just walls you know,' I say. That finally gets her attention. She looks at me and bites her lower lip.

'It's not. You know that. You know that better than anyone. Imagine all the women that were here when it was the Parramatta Girls Home or the asylum. Horrible things happened here, you know, really horrible.'

I'm listening to her speak and I'm watching the sun come in from behind the clouds and I'm thinking that this doesn't feel like the sort of place where horrible things could happen.

Mo lies down on her back and stares up at the sky. 'You know they say the place is haunted by all the women who lived here.'

She looks back at the house like she's looking for those women to show up and I watch her staring and say, 'I know. I think people come back when they need to. When they've still got stories they got to tell.'

Mo rolls over in the grass and leans her head against her elbow. 'There's a lot of stuff you know, don't you?' she says looking at me like I'm the new thing she's studying.

Caught

An almost empty apartment. A bright winter's day.
I'm lying on Mo's bed with her. She's so close I can feel her
all through my body even though we're not touching yet.

We're lying there looking up at the ceiling and Mo's
telling me about the places she wants to travel to one day
when she can. She tells me about the mosques in Dubai and
the pictures she has seen of their walls carved in patterns
on bright white cement. She tells me about this place she
wants to visit in India where everyone goes to pray and
bathe and send their dead people down the river. She talks
about the things she has seen in Egypt, pyramids made out
of rocks that look like sand, and about the pyramids they
have in other countries like Mexico; she'd like to go there,

Felicity Castagna

make comparisons. She's going to see all of these things one day but for now she's with me, on this bed.

When she flips on her side to look at me the sun from the window is throwing shadows over her face. She runs her finger from the top of my chin down to my belly button, like she could open me up. 'What are you thinking?' she asks.

'I don't know, just about you I suppose.' It makes me nervous when she asks me what I'm thinking. I don't think there's enough space in my brain to look at her body lying there and to make complete sentences at the same time.

So I move in. I run my hand from the top of her shoulder blade and down her side to her waist. She touches the back of my neck and I can feel her breathing slow and heavy in my ear. When I kiss her on the tip of her chin she goes silent. I move over on top of her lightly, afraid she might fall apart beneath me. We kiss and we touch all over the place. When I touch Mo, she feels like she's shaking against her own skin, on the inside.

When we stop kissing for a moment, that's when we both hear the doorbell ringing.

'Stop, stop,' she says lightly, pushing me off her. 'I don't know who that is, could be my brother's lost his keys.'

When I finally manage to get in touch with the real world again, I'm sitting up on her bed sweating.

And then it happens, her father walks straight in and stands there at the door to Mo's bedroom just staring at me with his enormous arms and waxy black hair and his broken-looking nose. Mo's standing next to him, looking like she wants to die and I'm waiting for everything to go silent and cut to another scene, like in the movies when the worst stuff is about to happen.

Nowhere to Go

I meet Mo in the stands and we watch her brother Joe attempt to play soccer. His dad made him join the team last week and Mo is trying to provide a bit of moral support. Joe isn't even trying, really. He's just standing at the edge of the field, straightening and pulling up his socks over and over again, like he's too busy to get involved in this silly game.

'You know, I'm not much of a soccer player but I could probably give Joe a hand, teach him to kick or something.'

Mo looks over and says, 'Yeh, maybe.' She bites the inside of her cheek and gives me a cold look. This morning she seems all twisted out of shape. She sits too far apart from me, one shoulder up and her arms crossed tightly.

'What's up?' I ask, looking at her, like I don't know what's up when we both know I do.

'My dad says, I can't see you anymore.'

'Right.' I don't know if I can lose anyone else. I've already lost enough this year.

'What if we don't tell him? We could just see each other without him knowing.'

'Nah,' she says, a kind of distance in her voice. 'He'll know. Everyone around here knows everything. No escape.'

Instead of replying, I grab her hand and she lets it sit in my palm for a moment, before pulling it away.

Dom in a Box

Mum lives in a daydream space between my brother's poster of Jessica Alba and the odd socks on his bedroom floor. This is what happens when you stop paying attention, when you can't move forward and still my mum is sitting there like she walked into a room and forgot what she was there for.

In a family like ours my mum's silence is so heavy you can feel it, like a thick doona lying over us. I sit down next to her on Dom's old bed. She has that box in front of her – Dom in a box; photographs and odd stuff. She puts the box on my lap and we start going through it together.

Here is a photo of him aged fourteen, looking cocky, his arms around his mates, the three of them standing in front of some field, legs apart, with their football jerseys on. Looking at him, I can see parts of myself in his stiff jaw and wild hair, in those deep-set eyes. In another image he is there, chucking a tantrum, throwing things on the floor. He looks at the camera, his lips folded into a grimace, as if he knows that there are terrible things to come. Elsewhere, a certificate with gold edges, something he won for having the best attendance in Year Five. I dig deeper and find a program for a play my brother was in. Boxes like this, these are the things that keep Mum's force-field around her, as strong as car windows that don't crack.

I put these parts of Dom back in their box and place it on the shelf and I look at Mum just sitting there with that blank face that doesn't show any kind of feelings any more and I want to get her out. Out of this bedroom, out of this apartment building, out of this suburb, 'Why don't we go for a walk Mum? Before dinner? We could walk around the park, or walk down to Dad's shop or something.'

She looks at me for a little while, her jaw all clenched up, her fists shoved tightly into her pockets and I realise for the first time that it's not just sadness, that she's got this anger inside of her that she can't let go of. 'Come on. Just a couple of times around the block,' I say, grabbing her arm, tugging it harder than I probably should.

'No,' she says and I want to shout at her, drag her out of this room but her voice has become deeper and cold.

'Fine,' I say and leave, even though I know I can't escape her. It's as useless as trying to escape your own shadow.

Photos

On the days when I imagine he's here, Dom is in the photograph I took that night we drove to the party in the East.

It's after the party. It's just me and him and we're at the Granville chicken shop. In the background of the photograph there is the street behind the shop glass. On the street there is the red-edge of a tail-light blurring into the white metal of the Pontiac Trans-Am. The car is a ghost car, it floats above the grey of the road like a space-ship that can't be held down to the ground.

On the other side of the glass, in the inside of the chicken shop there's Dom with his electric-blue eyes popping out of his head like someone's plugged him in. His face is tilted upward, his chin is sticking out. In his hand he's got a chicken sandwich. He looks like he's about to climb up onto one of the plastic tables and launch himself through the glass and out into the street where the cars are waiting for him.

Poof

Peter-puffer, Irish creamer, fruit, fairy, sodomite, butt-pirate, flaming shirtlifter, queen, pillow-biter, sausage-jockey, nancy, homo, knobgobbler.

To stop people from calling him gay, Joe always makes sure that he picks on other people before they can pick on him. The problem is he's not very good at picking on other people; he doesn't really do it the right way. Even when he's calling someone else gay it comes out sounding too soft and kind of girly. It only makes everyone tease him more.

I'm standing here with him at the bike gates because I told Mo I would, otherwise, I wouldn't be here; not in a million years. Shadi's standing ten feet away, mouthing, 'let's go' but I can't because Joe is farting off another stream of insults to some Year Ten kid about twice his size.

Joe has his bike handles gripped in his scrawny little hands and this other kid is kicking at his bike wheels so that Joe is having difficulty keeping it upright. 'Why ya got ta touch my stuff? Ya poof!' Joe is yelling in his high-pitched squeal and this other kid is laughing and pushing at his shoulder now so that Joe himself is about to topple over.

So I go and stand in between them and say, 'Alright we're going,' and I grab the front bar of Joe's bike before anyone, including him, has a chance to say anything. Joe walks alongside the bike between me and Shadi until we get to the school gates. At this point, he throws the bike on the ground and puts one hand on his hip and the other hand up in a gesture I'm sure I've seen in a Destiny's Child video clip. 'And don't you ever come near me again, homo,' he yells out towards the kid that was bugging him and we all run.

Mo in the Window

Mo is stuck there, looking out of the window on Friday and Saturday nights. She's stuck there, for now, because her father says she can't be trusted with me. I take the train to Granville and stand there underneath her window as if I'm Romeo in the play. Instead of the light of the sun and the moon and the stars and all that, there is the neon sign of her parents' shop advertising 'Fruit and Vegetables'.

She sits there on the window ledge with her stereo on, just looking at the sky with the window open, breathing out cold cloudy air like she's sitting in fog. I can hear her listening to Lady Gaga and Slipknot and singing along with the lyrics. Sometimes she drinks tea or sips on a can of Coke.

She won't acknowledge me standing down there until I start saying 'Hey Mo, hey.' At these times she makes paper aeroplanes with 'Shut Up' or 'Go Away' on their sides as if it was an airline logo and she shoots them straight down towards me, standing there, looking up at her.

Anger

'Where are you going?' Mum asks. She's got that angry clenched-jaw look again. She looks so small and fragile, like all that anger might just break her apart from the inside.

I shrug my shoulders and she hits me on the arm with the scrubbing brush from the kitchen sink. I keep walking and she follows after me. I pause for a moment, 'I'm just going to take a walk around the park or something, just need to get out.' Then I keep going towards the door again. She hits me on the back of the head with her scrubbing brush as I go. 'Will you stop?' Even in a rage Mum keeps her voice down now so it comes out sounding like an angry secret.

When I get to the front door I turn around and look at her standing there shaking the sink brush at me and I'm thinking that I don't know what to do with my face really, whether I should smile and say something like, 'Having a bad day?' or if I should look sad, sorry.

I'm trapped there in front of the door and she stops saying anything. She's just pulling at all the hairs in that sink brush until they fall out in her hands and drop to the floor in a white pile around her.

I was waiting for her to begin talking again but she doesn't and I'm trying to get together the right words but I can't. She always looks, these days, like she is about to begin saying something but she doesn't so I wait for what she might tell me. I wait to begin.

I can never work out the right words these days so I just say the same thing again, 'I'm just going out for a walk Mum,' and she pulls at the hairs of that brush for a while longer just staring at me like she doesn't recognise me or something.

Until she says slow and quiet, 'Suspended from school for cutting class and you think you can go off again, do whatever you want. I just want a little respect, a little rule following.'

But the sour look on Mum's face says this is not what she really wants. She wants me to not want to leave the house in the first place, to have not been suspended for cutting school. She wants things, lots of things beyond her control.

'Respect.'

'Rule following,' she says again and then she is off around the apartment outlining all the things she wants. She shows that she wants me to put away my own laundry by dumping a basketful of clothes on the floor. Looking pleased with her efforts she pushes the photograph albums off the shelf in the living room and then gets to pulling pots and pans out of the kitchen cupboards and letting them crash on the tile floor.

I watch her throwing everything around until she stops midway through dropping all the kitchen towels from the drawer to the floor, raises her head and looks at me like I've overstayed my welcome and says, 'Do whatever you want anyway,' before walking to her bedroom and slamming the door twice behind her.

When she's gone, I pick it all up carefully so that things don't make a sound when I put them back into the drawers. Then I slip through the front door and walk straight into the outside.

You do what you have to do

Outside, it's always strange that things are still the way they used to be. People just walk down the street, just like that, like my mum didn't throw everything in our house around as if it's normal.

I'm walking down the same street I've walked down my whole life and I'm thinking that the buildings should be in a different order today, or the trees in a different place. But they're not are they? Things just go on, so I walk down to Poppy's and he's sitting there on the plastic chairs on the lawn like usual, same as always. Sometimes he's with other guys from the home, sometimes he's talking to someone off the street, most of the time he's by himself. I sit down next to him and tell him what Mum's done now.

Poppy listens and nods his head. I tell him, 'I hope she doesn't break anything.'

'She'll do what she needs to do,' Poppy says as he leans back in his chair and watches the street.

Park Bench

Sometime, a long time ago, before Dom and I were even born, Mum carved her name into a wooden bench near the Parramatta Ferry Station. *Susan*. She must have carved it in really, really deep because it's still there. Sometimes when I want to think, I go down to the river and sit on that bench. I run my finger over those letters and watch the ferries come and go. It sorts my mind out.

I asked Mum why she wrote her name there all that time ago. She said that she wanted to mark her place in the world, so she knew where she was from, so that she could always get back there.

On not seeing Mo

I head out. Inside the house things are too quiet and too small. Mum and Dad and Poppy, Aunty Leena and even Sam are just sitting there watching the news, no one speaking, everyone sucking the air out of the place. I swear every time I exit and enter the living room it looks like the walls have inched themselves closer together. I don't even think anyone notices when I walk out the door.

I go down the stairwell past Esther's apartment, with its weak stream of TV light seeping out through the door and I head into the big biting wind. It's like I'm more awake than I've been in a long, long time. I don't know what to do with it sometimes; all this emptiness, so I walk. The apartment blocks have their own steady rhythm, their white glow. There is a comfort in walking, for almost a dozen blocks, I tell myself that I'm just getting some air. It isn't until I pass Harris Park Station and then Clyde, that I have to admit where I'm going.

By the time I walk over the pedestrian crossing that hangs over Granville station, it's late, real late, it's drizzling rain and there aren't that many people around. I watch these two guys leaning against the rail, sharing a cigarette, just hanging like they're waiting for some action. I walk down the main street, past the darkness of shops closed-up for the night and I head towards the 'Fruit and Vegetables' sign flashing like roadwork lights urging me forward with caution.

In her room, in that space above this world, the light is off in her window. I pull up a milk crate I find outside the shop and I sit there watching the space between us and I listen to the cars in the distance humming down the motorway.

An Outing with Aunty Leena

Friday afternoon, Aunty Leena takes me, Sam, Shadi and Sal out for ice-cream. She says ice-cream in winter puts hairs on men's chests. I'm not entirely convinced that anything will make hair start growing on my chest but I do appreciate ice-cream, wherever, whenever, at any time of year.

We head down to Cold Rock and Aunty Leena orders this thing that looks like a mountain of multi-coloured balls. It has nuts and hundreds and thousands and chocolate sauce and whip cream shoved in different places, toppling all over the plate and onto the table. This is Aunty Leena at her best, bigger than the whole world and not saying sorry for it. She takes the teaspoons the waitress has put on the table back to the counter and insists that they give us something more 'like a shovel'. She returns with five huge tablespoons and everyone gets into it. Sam ends up with a river of blue down the front of his shirt. Aunty Leena just shrugs and tells him that it would be a waste if more of the ice-cream didn't get into his mouth. Sal flicks her hair back and eats small mouthfuls of chocolate sauce and ice-cream and smiles at Shadi going for it with the full force of his Shadiness.

We all walk home down the river, drunk with ice-cream hangovers; even Aunty Leena struggles in her high, high boots. She draws me close to her, leans on my shoulder and says, 'Where's your girl?'

'Not allowed to see me anymore,' I tell her.

'Why?'

Because it is Aunty Leena, I let the whole story flow out around my feet. She nods and looks and listens while I talk and I love her for it, for the way she listens like everything you tell her has gravity.

'Right,' she says. 'I'll fix it.' And somehow I know she will, as we walk together, Aunty Leena clicking along in her heels.

Joe the Gangster

It's like everyone's God-given duty to piss Mr Alloshi off. And today, as always, Mr Alloshi is pissed. Not quite for the same reason that he was pissed this morning or yesterday or even an hour ago. This time he has an entirely new reason to be pissed and this time it's all about Joe. Mr Alloshi doesn't need to use the loudspeaker to find a boy. It's not his style. He walks through the playground at lunchtime casually asking where Joe is. This is how he plays it, even if he knows where you are, he just walks slowly towards you, asking everyone along the way with a look on his face like he's about to eat some poor boy and then spit his bones out so that by the time he gets to you, you already know, you're stuck in it real deep and there's no way out.

When I get the word, I'm over standing next to Joe, where he's pegging bits of bread at much bigger kids from the corner of the playground.

'What'd you do now?' I say, standing over him, wondering if Mo is worth the trouble of looking after her brother.

'No idea,' he says. He shrugs his shoulders and looks at the concrete and I think that he looks sad, deflated. For the first time in a long time, he doesn't look like he's up for a fight.

When Mr Alloshi arrives, the crowd of boys in front of us splits and it's just me and Joe standing there. Mr Alloshi points at Joe and then at me as well (in *The Rule Book of Mr Alloshi* people are guilty just because they stand next to other guilty people).

Like, five seconds later, we're in his office and Mr Alloshi picks up the *Daily Telegraph* and slams it down on his desk in front of us and then sits back in his big leather armchair, arms folded like he's done his work and he's just about ready to relax now.

And before I can work out what's going on, Joe turns into a jumping jellybean and he's all excited, pointing at his picture there on the front page. In the picture he's standing with half-a-dozen of the boys from his soccer team after a game at Lakemba Oval. Joe is grinning as though he's just won the lottery and the other boys are making faces like they're trying to look tough. They're all holding their hands up, making gangster signs. The type you see in the Tupac and Dr Dre videos.

The headline reads: *In Lakemba, Guns More Available than Pizza.*

Joe is still smiling when Mr Alloshi leans over his desk and says, 'Joe. Are you a gangster?'

'Umm…' Joe shifts in his chair waiting for the right answer to come out. 'No.'

'Do you purchase more guns than pizza?'

Joe laughs but quickly stops when he sees the look on Mr Alloshi's face. 'No,' he says, shaking his head left and right.

'So, why are you in this article?'

'Well, I don't know really. I was walking back to the train station after a game with a bunch of guys from my team and one of the streets was closed off and there were all these police and reporters so we went to have a look and then this lady, she walks up to us and starts asking if we're from the local area and if we, like, know people in gangs and how to get drugs and guns and stuff, so my mate Tom he says, "it's easier to get a gun than a pizza around here," and we all thought it was real funny so we started making signs like we were gangsters with guns and they started taking photos and so we just kept doing it.'

Mr Alloshi pushes his chair back and stands, leaning both arms over his desk and I'm thinking this is it, this is the moment when his head is really, truly, going to explode, but he just bites his bottom lip and looks at Joe real hard and says very slowly, 'So you just took it upon yourself to tell a bunch of lies and humiliate your whole community then?'

And Joe, unlike Joe, is completely stuck for words.

So Mr Alloshi, unlike Mr Alloshi, becomes very quiet-like and leans in very close and says. 'I find that very sad.'

I look at Joe and I can see the word 'sad' is floating over his head and he's just trying to catch it, draw it in and understand.

Learning Insults

This is Friday, the last lesson after lunch. This is after I help the boys throw Joe in the garbage can in the middle of the playground, after we take him out again, after we decide to put him back in, after we make guns out of our hands and pretend to shoot him, after Mr Alloshi walks onto the playground, after everyone runs away, this is after Mr Alloshi smiles at Joe in the garbage can and says he probably deserves it, this is after we wander into Mrs Morrison's English class.

Mrs Morrison, she looks at us and drops her hands to her sides. I can already see that she's giving up. She knows we aren't going to be reading any Shakespeare and pretending like it means something today. She sticks the end of her whiteboard marker in her mouth and looks at everyone coming in.

'Right,' she says and you can tell she's got an idea in her head. 'I was thinking that today, since it's Friday afternoon and we've all been studying so hard (a laugh from the classroom) we could learn some Shakespearean insults.' Mrs Morrison stands up and folds her arms and stares at us and we know it means we're supposed to shut up now and some of us do, and someone else coughs and says *faggot* into their hand and we all know that the cougher is talking about Shakespeare.

She hands out slips of paper ruled with three columns and explains that we need to start our insult with 'thou' and then combine one word from each of the columns in order to make our insult. She gives us an example by insulting Shadi in her nerdy Shakespearean way. She points her finger at him and says, 'Thou infectious doghearted codpiece.'

The boys get into it. Shadi points at me and says 'Thou coxcombed codfish harpy!' I laugh so hard I almost pee my pants. Mrs Morrison walks around the room saying, 'Good, give it to him.' But after a while, the boys trade other kinds of insults and I don't think she even notices the difference. Shadi teaches me to say '*Waj ab zibik*,' so I turn to Tom and spit it out all nasty-like at him, '*Waj ab zibik*, an infection on your dick.'

Tom is impressed. He teaches me how to say 'you son of a whore' in Italian, '*figlio di puttana*,' he shakes his hands in the air as he does this because that is how his grandfather always says it.

Darko overhears and stops stabbing Hugh in the leg with a pencil long enough to say, '*Sranje! Sranje!*' which his mother has told him is the worst thing you can possibly say in Serbian.

'Youse are a pack of bloody mongrels,' I say just like Poppy yells at the screen when he loses at the races.

Never Sure

When I get home Esther is in the hallway sweeping. 'Saw that girl of yours today,' she says and I'm thinking about all sorts of things and I almost miss what she's saying.

'Who?'

'Monique.'

'What? Where?'

'Just sitting out the front on the ledge by the mailboxes. I saw her out there this morning staring at the street. Then she was still there when I went out to check the mail a few hours later. So I said, "You waiting for Michael?" and she said she wasn't sure yet.'

'What do you mean she wasn't sure?' Esther just shrugs her shoulders and leans against her broom handle and looks at me. I want to grab her and shake her. 'Not sure about what?'

'You I suppose! Sometimes people need some time to work things out.'

Not sure, I say it to myself over and over again as I climb the stairs slowly to our apartment.

School Break

These September school holidays, Shadi and I spend a lot of time at the Granville servo. It's too cold out to go to the pool or the park or even the McDonald's parking lot. We stand in the sunlight, me, Shadi and Mohammed, the three of us leaning against the wall listening to the bells ringing in the Ukrainian church down the street.

Under Mohammed's instruction, me and Shadi can split a pumpkin seed between our teeth (most of the time) without choking ourselves to death. Next, Mohammed has promised he's going to teach us how to box. Already, he has hung the thick rubber base of an old chair up in the corner of the tiny staff-room. After eight, when the service station shuts down, he teaches us.

At this stage, we mostly just watch as Mohammed cuts through the air with his fists in one quick movement that brings his whole body forward against the cushion. Me and Shadi just sit there taking it all in, watching his stance, the way his feet float up and down on invisible cushions of air. He hits again and again but he never looks angry; he looks completely in control. Sometimes, when I'm watching Mohammed, I forget who he is for a second or two of blurry movement and I see Dom.

Shoes and Toes and Feet

Poppy and Sam are comparing their bare feet. They have the same crooked little toe on their left foot. Poppy's toes have long brown hair on them, Sam's are small and pink. Sam spends a lot of time looking at his toes and then at Poppy's before he finally puts his good socks on and then, his best shoes, the black ones just like Dom's; the Nike LEDs that light up and flash when you move around. Dad and Poppy have the same kind of shiny black leather Windsor Smiths that men get when they grow out of their Clark's cheap rubber school shoes. Dom had the type of shoes that were always lying on their sides in the middle of the floor. Mum always said *if you don't get those shoes out of the hallway*…but she never said what she would do and the shoes always stayed there.

I watch Poppy pick up his shoes and turn them over. There is a hole the size of a ten-cent coin in one and both of them have all their blackness rubbed out in the middle where they are mostly brown. I think of all the places he must have walked through in his life. He catches me looking and says, 'If you want to know who you are, watch your feet. Because where your feet take you, that's who you are.'

I look at my own feet and I think of how they look stuck there in the white sports socks I need to get around to taking off before I put my black school shoes on. All my feet do is remind me of how tied I am to the ground.

Visiting

Dad says that sometimes men need to do these things with other men. Poppy sits in the front seat and me and Sam are in the back. No one is speaking but you can tell that everyone's got their own thoughts going round and round in their heads.

We pull off the main road and go up through the big black gates yawning at us, open and wide. The whole landscape is different in here like you've suddenly arrived in another country. There are rows of palm trees on the roadside at first and then, later, old wild eucalyptus trees. We drive past the endless marble rectangles of Chinese letters like dominoes on one side and the rows and rows of crosses that change their shapes slightly as we pass the

Greek burial plots and the Serbians and then the Assyrians. The Italians, they build marble houses so big you can walk inside them and the Jewish people, they put stars everywhere so that their fields of black marble look like the night sky.

I can't help but think there must be a lot of people who wake up with the *there and not there* question on their minds.

We pull up in the Catholic part of the cemetery where the tombstones are guarded by statues of saints and angels watching over them. Dad walks at the head of the line followed by me and Sam and Poppy.

Dom's place is different from before. The simple white cross and the raised mound of earth have been replaced with a marble headstone and a flat patch of grass. It all looks more permanent now.

Dad shoves his hands deep into his pockets and goes silent like he just doesn't have the energy to say anymore. He moves forward slightly and bows his head and you know he's talking to Dom in his own quiet way.

Poppy leans close to me and Sam and says that we should think of what we want to say to Dom now that we're here with him. But all I can think is, *Dom's not here.* He'd never stay in such a still place with all these trees and everyone silent underground. If he's anywhere he's back on Church Street, watching the cars slide by.

Sam tugs at my hand and I am brought back to where

we are again. In front of me, my father isn't what he's been trying to be over the past year. He doesn't look smiling or hopeful any more. Instead, he's turned into a stream, just pouring out there, his big hands not enough to hold back the tides falling down his face.

We get up close to him, me and Poppy and Sam and hold him, so he knows he's not alone and all four of us become a river, right there, pouring our grief into each other.

Socks

It has rained socks again, overnight. I sit on the balcony with Mum and we look at the small yellow one stuck in the tree branch and I wonder if the little girl upstairs has cold feet. Mum picks up the blue-and-red-striped sport sock that has fallen onto our balcony railing and holds it in her hand.

I get up and look over the balcony where Esther is standing on the pavement holding up a pair of stockings and I wave.

Boxing

We're standing in the petrol station again, for the fourth night in a row after closing time, learning how to box from Mohammed. Shadi leans up against the shelf where the motor oil is kept, looking like he's going to burst with all this concentration. Things are quiet. I fold my arms across my chest and watch the old cushion swaying backwards and forwards on its rope, spitting pieces of fluff from the places where it's falling apart.

Mohammed says, 'The way you hit can show what sort of person you are; it shows if you're not sure enough about yourself, if you've got too much anger, if you're the sort of person who gets knocked and never gets up again.'

He puts his gloves on and does another demonstration

of how to hit, he throws himself into it, skin, muscles, breath, they all come out in one straight punch. The cushion swings and hits the ceiling. He catches it again on its way down.

Next, it is my turn. Mohammed takes off his gloves and hands them to me. They are heavy in my hands, like carrying someone's head. On the inside they feel like you're slipping your fists into an old pair of socks.

Mohammed stands behind me, pulls my shoulders back and says to relax my body, to stop tensing my muscles. 'To box,' he says, 'you have to feel like you're comfortable in your own skin.'

I let go, swinging my right arm and then my left into the cushion. I try lifting up my feet slightly, bouncing them on and off the ground until it makes me feel like I'm floating. I punch with my left arm and then with my right again. And I'm hitting it again and again and I get it, the way you can lose yourself, skin, muscles, breath. I let myself go.

When Mohammed grabs the cushion and makes it stop, I know I've been gone too long. He stands there, wrapping his arms around it, nodding his head up and down slightly. 'Yeh,' he says and nothing more about it but I know he thinks I've done alright. 'Step back now and let Shadi have a turn. Take a breath, take a deep breath,' he says and I realise how low and heavy I'm breathing in and out but it's a different kind of heavy now, not as heavy as it's been all year. The sound of me heaving in and out fills the storeroom.

Shadi hands me his drink bottle and I take a sip in between breaths. Mohammed leans over me and smiles 'You can't give all your energy away at once in the ring, you've got to hold back a little, so you've got a little bit of something in reserve,' he says.

Eels

Five minutes after I get the invite from Shadi, Dad is driving me over there. 'Did you know,' I tell him, 'if they win, the Premier is going to paint two trains in Parra colours and name them the Hayne Train and the Fuifui Moimoi Express?'

Dad nods, 'That's a lot of paint.' Dad doesn't know much about this stuff and I'm not sure he's so interested but he always wants to know what I'm interested in. Besides, he couldn't help being a little curious with everyone going mad around here now that the Eels are actually winning and have made it to the Premiership.

Once we hit Church Street we are stuck in this maze of unmoving cars for forty minutes. The gates to the stadium don't open for another two hours but everyone's already out in force, they're crowding the streets and sitting in the stadium car park.

The big game is on everyone's face. They mime football poses as they walk down the street, they hang flags out their car windows and wear their blue and gold jerseys, they have their faces painted in enough zinc to last them right through to next summer.

We're sitting there stuck and some kid in the car next to us waves and slaps a poster of Fuifui against the window. 'Who's that?' Dad laughs getting caught up in it all, in everything.

'It's Fuifui, Dad. He's like a god.'

In the car next to us two women wearing blue and gold headscarves are waving an Eels flag out their car window.

'Does Shadi think that Fuifui is God?'

'No. He thinks Jarryd Hayne is more of a god and Shadi's sister likes Daniel Mortimer because all girls are in love with Daniel Mortimer.'

This trip looks like it's going to take as long as life itself.

I turn on the radio and like a teenager Dad turns it up on high and sticks his arm out the window and we slide along watching all those people in their blue and gold.

Shadi's House

Dad drops me off at Shadi's house. This house with all its Greek pillars and marble, looking like it should be in Europe somewhere, not in Merrylands. Shadi's younger sister Jen opens the door and shows me to the living room like she's been doing for ever even though she knows I know the place. I go and sit in there, with all its neon-coloured daisies on the cushions and bright red leather sofas.

Jen is playing with the colour and tone buttons on their giant TV, just trying to get it perfect. 'Better or worse?' she keeps saying to me like an eye doctor. She's got her hair tied up with blue and gold ribbons but she hasn't tied it up real good and her hair is falling all over her face.

'Better?' I say but I'm not so sure. Shadi's mum's into

those Jesus heads that light up and rotate and the pictures of the Virgin Mary with the back lighting. Between the corner of the living room where she keeps these things on a table and the red leather sofas and the white, white tiles, there's too much colour in front of me and everything is getting all mixed up.

'Better or worse?' Jen says, looking at me real hard like she wants to make sure I'm not lying.

I can hear Shadi in the kitchen with his mum. He's saying 'Yes, Mum,' again and again and she's giving him a list of the things we're allowed to do and not to do while she and Shadi's dad go out tonight.

Shadi finally makes it into the living room but his mum's still talking at him. 'Did you hear what I said?' I hear her shout from the kitchen.

'Got it,' Shadi yells before he drops down on the couch so hard he almost knocks me off. He's got his Eels scarf on and his Eels beanie, even though it's getting a bit too warm for that now. In his right hand he's got a long blow-up balloon in blue and gold and he's using it to whack Jen who's lying on her stomach five inches from the TV going 'Shadi, Shadi, stop it.'

Shadi's mum walks through the living room with his dad. She's got this bright green dress on and she says, 'How do I look boys?' And we shrug our shoulders and she rolls her eyes and Shadi's dad looks at the TV like he's drooling and you know he doesn't want to go out.

And then, at last, they're out the door and Shadi and Jen are in the cupboards pulling out homemade pastries and biscuit tins and Coke. Jen arranges the goods on the living-room table in front of the TV like we are going to a picnic.

Shadi turns on the plasma and unplugs all his mother's glowing statues of the Virgin and the rotating Jesus heads so they don't cast any images on the screen and then we're ready and waiting to watch our own gods on the football field.

Esther's Walls

This morning, Esther wants to paint her walls. Dad and I are leaning over the balcony as the guy from Bunnings goes back and forth between his van and Esther's apartment with big cans of white paint. Esther is just standing there all hunched over with her hands on her hips and her hair pulled tightly back in a bun on the top of her head. She's got the type of floral dress on she only wears when she is going out.

'That woman gets crazier all the time. How's she going to paint her apartment?' Dad says to me, quietly. I can't even imagine how Esther could lift a paint can. We watch as Esther pulls out her purse and gives the man a two-dollar coin for all his help.

I go downstairs to Esther's apartment. Her door is open. I can hear a screeching sound like moving furniture. She doesn't hear me when I knock on the door so I just let myself in. Inside, she's moving cans of paint towards the different walls of her apartment by kicking them with her feet.

'Hey Esther,' I say and she stops suddenly and looks up at me all startled-like.

'Come in, come in,' she says. We're going to paint. We're getting ready for spring.'

And before I can ask who he is, this thin, tall man with long arms and legs like Spiderman emerges from the kitchen. He's got Esther's eyes, the type that look like they're pushed a little too far into someone's head. He's standing quietly, looking at me like he's not so sure how he got here.

'This is my son Tom,' Esther says before going back to kicking paint cans towards the walls as if it is the most normal thing in the world that this man, who has never been let in before, has suddenly turned up to paint.

'Hi,' Tom says. He shakes my hand as if he's nervous. 'Mum always talks about how good the boys upstairs are.'

'Well, no sense in wasting time, let's get to it,' Esther says.

I help Tom stick newspapers to the edges of the floor. He moves quickly like he's done this all before, never saying anything just getting into it. Esther sits in a chair giving instructions. She looks more than pleased with herself today. She looks glowing. I notice that she has makeup on – bright pink lipstick and globs of powder sitting in her wrinkles. She wears the dress she reserves for Sundays and folds her hands neatly in her lap.

Esther hands us sponges bigger than my head and Tom shows me how to get the walls ready for painting by rubbing them with sugar soap. I scrub into the walls hard and watch them lose some of their greyness.

Esther brings us super-sweet tea and biscuits on a tray. 'We're starting new,' she says picking up her good china teacup and holding it tight in her hand.

Last Meeting

Whatever else happens there is always making out with Mo. Mo is telling me the story of Aunty Leena arriving at the fruit shop and charming her father into letting me back into Mo's life. I am trying to listen. I am half-listening but I get distracted by her pink lip-gloss.

The sun falls like goo through the trees and spills all over one side of Mo's face. She puts her whole fist into the pocket of my jacket and pulls her lips away from mine. Her face; that look – I can't explain it but it just makes my insides feel right. Mo twists her hair around her index finger and rolls over on the grass.

And we lie there, still, for most of the afternoon, in a quiet spot by the edge of the lake. Mo looks up at the sky and points at the clouds. 'That one to the left, that's your Poppy on his motorcycle, those two long clouds together, that's me floating beside you at the swimming pool next summer like two fish in the sea.'

This time of year, almost the end of spring and the promise of warm weather and shorter skirts is just around the corner. I move over closer to Mo so that I can feel her leg up tight against mine. I look up at the clouds and I point out things too. 'That's the window of your bedroom, that's the apple stand in front of your parent's shop. That's the car I'm going to get one day to drive you around in.'

No one can tell that
woman what to do

I take Mo out for charcoal chicken. It's our thing now, like before it was me and Dom's thing but now it's also a me and Mo thing.

Mo is the only person I know who eats charcoal chicken with a knife and fork in tiny little bites like she's at some fancy restaurant and not in Granville. She takes another bite and smooths back the frizz on her head by rubbing her palm across it.

The place is warm and chicken-smelling. I watch her do her thing with the knife and the fork and the pickles. She looks her best when she's not noticing you noticing her. She puts the knife and fork down and bites her thumb nail and looks at me.

'Why did you come to my apartment block that day and not come in?'

'What?'

'You came to my apartment building and sat outside with the mailboxes. Esther said you didn't come up because you weren't sure.'

'Mmm…I wasn't sure. Should I listen to my dad and not hang out with you or should I listen to you saying I should ignore my dad or should I just not listen to both of you so that I can decide what I really want.'

'What did you decide?'

'I decided to listen to what I want,' she says as she folds her arm across her chest and keeps on looking at me straight in the face and smiling and smiling.

Dreams

I have a dream where Dom is here. He's all see-through like a ghost and he's got this glow about him like a tail-light. I open up the car door for him and he gets in the car and says, *drive*. We are glowing purple. We speed up and brake, sliding over concrete like primo-star ice-skaters, Dom with his arm hanging out the window, scanning for girls and me trying to look all relaxed like I'm him, like I'm ready for the world to just keep coming and coming, Dom by my side again.

The Incredible Here and Now

Only four people are left in this apartment now and everyone moving around it in their own ways; Dad, Poppy, me, walking around Mum's silence.

I decide to take Mum out for a walk. The trees have grown back their leaves and it's a good time for walking. I hold her, my arm under hers, walking her like a gentleman, like Dom used to. I tell her the stories behind all the places we pass. When we walk past the alleyway, I tell her about the night that Dom and I sat in the car, watching Esther's son in the gutter. We walk through the park past the tombstones and I hold her hand and I tell her about the magazines and where the good china pot that Dom broke is buried.

This whole place, it's just a bunch of people's

memories bubbling up from the ground, spilling out of the buildings all the time. The good thing about telling those stories is that the feelings all come back to you. Under my arm I can feel my mum disappearing, closing herself off but I don't let her go.

We walk on past the Bread-Shop Man and the store with the bootleg DVDs and the Vietnamese grocer who always has boxes of sweetened condensed milk. I tell her the stories behind all these places as we go. I tell her about the raging crazy summers of ice-coffees and watching *The Fast and The Furious* dubbed in Chinese and then it happens and I know, if it's not a sign from God, then it's got to be a sign from Dom.

That pearly white Pontiac Trams Am drives past us slowly, the driver with his arm stuck out the window, and I put my arm around Mum and make her face the street and I say, 'And the story behind that car, that's definitely Dom.'

Underneath my arm she falls apart. She is weeping. Like the neighbourhood, she is uncontrollable. This place is carrying on like it can't stop it. Girls, they're pouring out of shops in their short dresses and the boys, they're still in the McDonald's parking lot watching the whole world go by, and people are getting up early in the morning, putting on their bests, heading off for their churches, their mosques, their temples. And I can see it, I feel it.

Sometimes, I wish we could go back to the beginning of the story, before ice-skating, before cars. But you can't go back. There's only moving forward so I put my arm around Mum's shoulder and I tell her about the incredible here and now.

Acknowledgements

Firstly, I would like to thank the Westside Writers' Group where this book was born and raised. So many of the group's members gave me the generous feedback and support that has made this book possible. It has been an honour working with such talented writers over the years and I look forward to having that great pleasure in the future. Thanks to; Michael Mohammed Ahmad, Susie Ahmad, Hasan Bajis, Arda Barut, Kavita Bedford, Lachlan Brown, Luke Carman, Tamar Chnorhokian, Samantha Hogg, Lina Jabbir, Andy Ko, Rebecca Landon, Peta Murphy, Benny Ngo, Francis Panopoulos, Peter Polites, George Toseski, Randa Sayed, Nitin Vengurlekar, Fiona Wright and Amanda Yeo.

Many thanks to the Australia Council for the Arts for

its award of an Emerging Writers' Grant, buying me much needed time to work on this manuscript in its early stages. I would also like to acknowledge the support I received from The Varuna Writers' Centre, through their Publishers' Fellowship Program. In particular I would like to thank Deb Westbury for her feedback and encouragement on my manuscript.

Ivor Indyk, thank you for your continued support and your greatly detailed edits, which have made this a much stronger book. Alice Grundy, thank you for your support during the publishing process.

Maria Boyd gave me every ounce of her patience one afternoon at her kitchen table as she went through my manuscript with me page by page. Thank you for your eye for detail and voice and for all your great conversations about writing.

Thanks go as well to many others who have given me feedback on sections of this book; Pip Smith, Ronny Habib, Etuate Talanoa, Kath Faniki and Louisa Li.

Thank you to Libby Gleeson for generously giving her time to reading my manuscript and providing a quote for the back of the book.

To the Parramatta Marist and St Mary's boys, you're all here somewhere in this book. Thank you for being my teacher and for allowing me to see how complex and incredible the lives of young men really are.

As always, thank you to my family for their support

over a lifetime, especially to my parents Tony and Sandy and my brother Adam.

And last but never least, to my husband, Michael, who lovingly read the drafts of this book and who is always my greatest support.

This project has been assisted by the Commonwealth Government through the Australia Council, its arts funding and advisory body.

Felicity Castagna spent her youth living and travelling around Asia and North America before moving to Parramatta, where she has worked as a teacher, arts worker and editor for the past ten years. Her collection of short stories *Small Indiscretions* (Transit Lounge, 2011) was highly praised. She has won the Josephine Ulrick Literature Award and the Qantas Spirit of Youth Award.

Teaching notes available from
www.giramondopublishing.com